Love Notes

SUSAN SCOTT SHELLEY

DEDICATION

To Jacqueline Jayne.
Here's to friendship!

ACKNOWLEDGMENTS

First and foremost, thank you to my amazing husband. You truly were a rock star during the writing of this book. I love you.

Thank you to my beta reader/brainstormer crew: Jackie, Tina, Chantal, and Beth. You all are completely wonderful! I cannot thank you enough.
.

CHAPTER ONE

Home.

Finally.

Zander Rostov drove through the gates of his estate and coasted up the long drive, relieved to be surrounded by the hush of his own paradise. The exhaustion of the last few months on tour weighed heavy on his bones. Too much time cooped up with his band, too much in-fighting, and too many late nights and early rises left him itching for solitude and hours of sound sleep.

Beside him, his English Bulldog snored. What a life—eat, sleep, play, repeat. Lucky dog. But for the next two weeks, he'd have a taste of it, too. Two weeks to breathe before the chaos began all over again. A small piece of freedom, enough to tease him before being thrown back into six weeks of shows and travel. After ten years of near-constant recording and touring, he needed a break. A long break—from the band, from the grind, and from the lingering frustration he hadn't been able to shake for months.

When he parked the car, Shredder roused with a pitiful grumble, his overbite pushing his bottom lip into a pout.

"We're home, buddy." Zander rubbed the dog's

brown and white wrinkled head. He took his pet on the road with him as often as he could. Seven-years-old and content to laze around, his bulldog made the perfect travel companion. He opened the passenger door and Shredder bounded off across the lawn, protected by the eight-foot-high walls surrounding the Spanish Mission-style home, his just-private-enough retreat from the world.

A breeze rustled the palm trees. The beginning of April in Santa Monica was warmer than the end of March in New York City had been. The east coast tour had ended in the city that never sleeps and then eight hours later, he'd parted ways with his band mates who never seemed to get along anymore. The break wasn't really a break, with the few press events and the party for the fans lined up.

Stretching, he breathed in deep and fought down the urge to throw the bags back in the car, grab the dog, and just take off. Years of saying yes to everything had drained him dry but he couldn't disappoint the fans. The success of the tour and the new album were more important than his need to recharge, even if the last few months had been the most difficult of the band's career.

He left the dog in the garden and entered the house. Cool air and silence greeted him. He set down his guitar case in the living room, then dropped his luggage on the floor outside the laundry room. He'd unpack before his housekeeper arrived. Settling the dog with food and water came first. Man's best friend deserved a reward after hours of travel. The next part of the tour would be easier—all in California, and several local shows. When he needed to be away for a few days, his housekeeper would watch Shredder or the dog would stay with his parents.

The ping of an email alert made him reach for his phone. The sender—Oliver Somers from Excite Records—could wait long enough for him to have a cold one. He let Shredder in, then cracked open the beer and downed half the contents. Oliver's email started off with the usual pseudo-friendly nonsense, then listed the upcoming tour dates. At the very end, the son-of-a-bitch had tacked on an additional two weeks' worth of shows.

Fuck!

He crushed the can in his fist. Beer sloshed over his hand and splashed the kitchen floor. Shredder trotted over and licked at the puddle.

"Damn it, no." He grabbed the dog's collar and tugged him away.

Two weeks... The burn of anger singed his muscles. He slammed his fist onto the counter, then hurled the can into the sink. Metal clattered and Shredder whimpered and hid under the table.

Fuming, he wiped the spill and then sat on the floor, staring at the dog. He needed to hold it together. He rubbed his palms over his face and forced his muscles to relax. Calling for the dog, he reached for his phone.

He'd left his sister an hour ago and Irisa hadn't said a word about more tour dates. As band manager, the discussion of more tour dates should have come from her. Which meant Oliver had once again overstepped his authority. His muscles tightened again. With the dog curled onto his legs, he dialed Irisa's number.

It rang several times before her voice came on the line. "What's up? You should be sleeping."

"Check your email. Excite added a few more venues to the tour."

"What?" Her voice hardened. "Oliver knows that's supposed to be cleared with me first."

"I'm not happy about it either. We're fucking exhausted and they go and add in five more shows to the end of the tour, with maybe more to come. We'll be working through the whole summer at this rate."

"I'll make it clear that he can't add on any more. I'll start looking at hotels." She sounded as worn out as he felt. He knew she didn't like Oliver any more than he did. The jerk had used her to get his job—something Zander couldn't forget.

He rubbed Shredder's head. "I can help."

"I'll handle it. Don't worry. Get some sleep. I'll call you when I've figured it out."

Sleep was out of the question. He hurled dirty clothes into the washer, then reached for the only thing that ever settled him—his guitar. Time didn't exist when he played. Nothing existed except the music. He heard about it often enough from his sister, so he set his phone on the table, where he'd be sure to see her call.

He didn't know how long he'd been playing when the phone's ringing jarred him out of his relaxed mood. He saw texts from his band mates, probably ticked off about the added dates. Ignoring them, he answered his sister's call.

"Travel and hotels are all set. Listen, I've hired

my friend Jayne to help me out during the tour. I've told you about her, she's a tour manager, and really, after how you guys have been, I need someone to keep me sane."

His sister did so much for them, allowing them to focus on the music and the fans. "Hey, if you want to bring someone along, that's fine. Whatever you need."

"She wants to meet you all first before she'll take the job. I know you're tired, but please? A quick meeting this afternoon. Four o'clock, at the coffee shop by your house."

"Fine. Did you call the guys?"

"Yes, they'll be there."

"Then I'll see you at four." He clicked off.

Hmmm. Jayne Warren.

He'd never met Jayne, but from pictures he'd seen at his sister's place and from all Irisa had said about her friend, he felt like he knew her already. Jayne Warren, a gorgeous blonde with eyes nearly the same shade of blue as his favorite guitar.

When he walked into the coffee shop a few hours later, his band mates Luke, Landry, and Brendan, sat at a table in the back of the nearly empty room.

Luke raised his brow. "You live the closest but you're the last one here."

He shrugged. "So? I'm here now."

"We only got here a few minutes ago anyway, Thompson." Landry shook his head at Luke, then sipped his coffee.

"Whatever. I don't understand why we had to meet this girl today. This could've waited a few days."

"Maybe it couldn't have waited. Where else did you need to be? My sister said it'll be quick, so it'll be quick. Calm the hell down." Zander turned at the sound of the door opening.

Irisa walked in, followed by Jayne. She was far more beautiful than the pictures he'd seen.

The classic oval face, high cheekbones with a hint of color, wide ocean-blue eyes fringed by thick lashes, sculpted brows, and full lips, petal pink and perfect for kissing. She was taller than his sister. A quick estimate suggested the top of her head would reach right under his chin if he held her close. She glided toward them—long limbs, delicate curves, and the graceful moves of a dancer. Rather than the platinum blonde hair she'd had in the photos, strawberry blonde locks tumbled over her shoulders in thick waves. His hands itched to sink in and test the weight.

Her gaze met his. Something within him clicked, shifted, then settled.

With the sexy bombshell along for the ride, maybe he'd survive the tour after all.

***

Jayne's pulse fluttered as she held Zander's gaze. If she hadn't been heading his way, his warm hazel eyes alone would have pulled her toward him. When Irisa had asked her to come along for the California leg of the tour, and promised her double her usual salary, she hadn't thought about how attractive Zander was, or how her body responded on the rare occasions he took over lead vocals on a song. She hadn't thought past how the money would go a long way toward fixing her bank account, or how working might be just the thing to help her regroup after Pepper's death. She missed her dog more than anything.

Now was not the time to dwell on that. She followed Irisa's path and came to a stop in front of one of rock's biggest bands. After spending years backstage and seeing rock stars at their best and worst, not much fazed her. But her heartbeat wouldn't calm.

Zander stood next to the table. Up close, his eyes were more brown than green. A shadow of stubble highlighted his square jaw and chiseled cheekbones, and led to thick brown hair, short at the sides and back, just a bit longer on top, and messy enough for her to want to smooth the strands. His slightly crooked nose and muscular build behind worn jeans and a snug gray t-shirt suggested a boxer rather than a musician. Maybe the comparison wasn't quite so far-fetched. Both boxers and musicians were talented with their hands. Her gaze dropped to his wide palms and long fingers. A shiver zinged up her spine. Imaging his hands on her was too easy.

"Let me introduce you, then we'll grab some coffee." Irisa touched her shoulder. "Guys, this is Jayne Warren."

Dragging her gaze from Zander, Jayne smiled at the other men. "Hello."

"This is Landry, our bassist." Irisa pointed to the guitarist with a shock of espresso-colored hair.

Known to be the most stoic of the group, he nodded at her.

"Brendan, our drummer." Sporting a beard and shaggy brown hair, the drummer was famous for his light gray eyes and easy sense of humor. He offered her an easy smile.

"Luke, our lead singer." With the brooding good looks millions of women adored, he didn't react at all.

"And my brother Zander, lead guitar." His brow quirked and his gaze roamed her face, settling for just a second too long on her lips. When she licked them, his eyes jumped back to hers.

"It's nice to meet all of you. I've been a fan for years."

"She's worked with Glitter Breeze, Bald Cracker, and Metro Danger." Irisa ticked the names off on her hand. "And I'm so happy to have her with us."

"I'm looking forward to working with you guys."

Luke stood, looming over her. "Look, sweetheart. This isn't going to be like handling one of those little bands. We're The Fury."

Blinking, she stared at him while her mind worked on what to say. Her stomach felt like someone had punched her. After Irisa's pleading that she come on board, she didn't think she'd have to prove her merit, and she hadn't expected Luke's hostility.

"Whoa, hold up there." Zander shifted closer, putting himself between her and the singer.

Irisa shot Luke a glare. "She's good. I wouldn't

have hired her if I didn't think she could handle it. Believe me, I need my job to be less stressful, not more."

The image of her much smaller friend lecturing a man nearly a foot taller than her would have been comical, if the situation hadn't been so awkward. Irisa's support helped, but the rest of the bands she'd worked with, those on the same level as The Fury, would help more. Lifting her chin, Jayne looked him in the eye. "I've also worked with The Never Theory, Toxic Stand, and Vendetta. Feel free to contact them."

Zander moved into her space, blocking her view of his grumbling band mate. He extended his hand. "Welcome aboard."

"Really?" Her palm slid across his. A sizzle shot along her arm when the calloused pads of his fingers brushed her skin.

"Really." His fingers closed around her hand and his eyes sparked with heat. Then he sent a glare at Luke and his hold tightened a fraction more.

His scent—the leather jacket and some type of musky cologne made her head spin. She inhaled slow and deep to quiet her fluttering heartbeat. His hand still held hers. Swallowing hard, she loosened her hold.

His lips formed a half smile and he slowly released her hand. The glittering in his eyes held a promise of hot kisses and wild nights. Her pulse thrummed in her ears.

Dangerous.

Absolutely dangerous.

And she couldn't get involved. Clients were

firmly in the off-limits category.

"Come on, let's put in our order." Irisa bumped her elbow. "Or, do you know what you want? I'll get it."

She glanced from Luke to Zander. They stood, squaring off with nearly identical intimidating expressions. Tension thickened the air. "I'll, ah, come with you."

When they reached the counter, Irisa leaned in close. "I'm sorry. They're just tired. It's been a long tour."

"Are you sure? Luke seems like he thinks I can't handle things."

"He's really a nice guy, I promise." She bit her lip, then placed her order and waited for Jayne to do the same.

Fifteen minutes earlier, she'd been brimming with excitement over the tour and working with Irisa. Now, as she lingered over adding cream and sugar to her coffee, her enthusiasm had vaporized and she struggled to compose herself.

Heated words in low tones flew between Luke and Zander. Something about the band needing to be fully on board in making decisions, and Zander telling Luke to calm the hell down. Landry leaned toward the pair, and whatever he said earned a curt "Fuck you" from Luke.

Jayne winced. Maybe she should just back out now. Artists could be temperamental but Luke's reaction confused her. Maybe he really was afraid she'd screw up. Luke's reaction aside, the guys were too tense. Yes, they had just finished months of touring and flown home on the red-eye, but still…

Brendan met her gaze. He gestured to the empty seats at the table, one in between him and Landry, right across from where Luke stood. "Join us."

That was the last place she wanted to be. "I think I better go."

"No. Wait, please." Irisa strode past her, right into the line of fire. "Guys, come on now. We're all tired but we have two weeks to relax and sleep in our own beds. And there's plenty of days off where we'll be at home during the next two months. This should be easy compared to Europe, Canada, and the East Coast. Please, let's start this leg off on a good note."

"Fine." Zander moved away from Luke and closer to Jayne. In a flash, his scowl vanished and that sexy smile reappeared. She answered that smile with one of her own.

"I'm out." Luke tossed his cup into the trash and then slammed out of the shop.

"I'm his ride home, you'd think he'd wait for me." Landry stood and shrugged into his leather jacket. "This was productive. See you guys on Tuesday."

"What's Tuesday?" Jayne gripped her cup. Steam curled up in a ring. The rich coffee and hazelnut scents calmed her despite the tension with the band.

"A party with some fans who won a contest. Maybe Luke will have the bug out of his ass by then." With that, the bassist left.

Brendan drained his cup. "I guess I'll head out too. Maybe I've over-caffeinated enough that I'll actually sleep." He stood and gestured again for Jayne to sit. "Welcome to the tour."

"Thanks." She returned his wave. Zander walked with him toward the door. The welcome seemed to be split. Zander and Brendan for her, Luke against, and she couldn't get a read on Landry.

Irisa settled into the seat beside Jayne. "They're exhausted."

"So you said." But looking at Irisa's earnest expression, she couldn't back out. Not after all Irisa had done for her over the years, especially during Pepper's illness.

Zander returned, carrying a coffee. He flipped a chair around to face Jayne, then straddled it and shrugged. "I'll apologize for Luke."

"You don't have to do that."

"Yeah, I do. My band, my responsibility. I don't want you feeling bad because my singer is an idiot."

His expression bordered on frustrated and annoyed. She slipped into the mode she knew best—the fixer. "Don't worry, I'm fine."

"So you're definitely in? You'll help me?" Irisa leaned forward, coffee forgotten.

"I'm in."

Zander reached across the table, extending his hand. A smile formed on his lips and that dark expression lightened. "Shake on it?"

Jayne slid her hand against his. The strength of his grip ignited the same response as the first time they'd touched. Hopefully her decision wouldn't come back to burn her.

.

CHAPTER TWO

Zander sat in his bedroom, hyped up on the coffee he shouldn't have consumed. Picturing Jayne, he picked out notes on his guitar. Playing always calmed him, distracted him, but he couldn't relax. She'd looked so sexy and sweet standing in that coffee shop. The little leather jacket, the snug jeans, the pale pink nails and matching lips. His body tightened. But she hadn't seen the band at their best. Luke had been an asshole. Not that the rest of the guys had been much better. She'd looked so unsure when they'd said goodbye.

He dialed his sister's number. She could give him Jayne's number and then he'd… Say what? Apologize? Make sure she knew they didn't usually act that way? He couldn't lie. He could say, *if you'd been with us last year, we were getting along better then*. That wouldn't do a lot of good. Damn it, he didn't want to scare her off.

A woman hadn't drawn his interest so completely in ages. He was damn tired of being alone. The years of constant recording and touring hadn't been kind to relationships. Too often in his business, he'd seen relationships go down in flames because of jealousy, long absences, infidelity, or suspected infidelity. And one night stands weren't his style. He'd resigned himself to being alone…but then she'd walked into that coffee shop and all he could think about was her.

Irisa's voicemail picked up. Before he could leave a message, an incoming call alert sounded. Thinking it was his sister, he engaged the call.

"Zander." Luke's voice slurred through the speaker.

"What?" He barked the word. Fresh annoyance tingled along his skin.

"I, ah, got arrested."

Shit. So not what the band needed right now. "What the hell did you do?"

"Boating. Drinking. Drinking while boating."

"Are you serious?" Luke had always taken care to follow rules when out on his boat. "What happened?"

"Obviously I had a little too much to drink." The slurring exaggerated his sarcastic tone.

"Was anyone with you?"

"No. They won't release me until tomorrow."

"Good, then hopefully we have at least that long before the press finds out." He jotted down the police station's number, listened to Luke ramble for another minute, then ended the call.

Fucking hell. He hated seeing anyone lose control. What a way to kick off the tour. The band wasn't any stranger to partying, but they'd gotten the worst of it out of their systems earlier in their career. Now, they had too much at stake to take stupid chances.

He called his sister again and relayed the news. She'd start damage-control. He pushed away the idea of calling Jayne. Why bother her when he didn't have any idea what the hell would happen with Luke or how it would affect the tour.

Early Monday morning, after a weekend filled with too much press, he dodged some reporters hoping for a sound bite and entered the courthouse with his sister. He sat cooling his heels in a hallway with Brendan and Landry while Luke and his lawyer waited for sentencing. Irisa had suggested they all show up for moral support, but Luke's lawyer had two security guards block them from following Luke into the court room. Apparently his lead singer didn't want or need their presence. His annoyance grew with every passing minute. After an hour, Zander pushed to his feet. This was ridiculous. He was about to tell the guys he was taking off when the door opened and Luke emerged—his face expressionless, dressed in a suit and tie.

Irisa leapt to her feet. "Well?"

"I have to pay a fine and do thirty hours of community service."

"We don't have to miss any tour dates?"

"No. But I won't have my license for six months. So I guess one of you will be driving me around." His gaze connected with Zander, then moved to the other guys.

"Of course, whatever you need." Irisa placed her hand on his arm.

Like hell. Zander kept quiet. Brendan and Landry did too. Irisa aimed a glare at them over her shoulder. "I'm sure the guys are more than happy to help out, too."

Luke lifted a brow. "Sure. I can hear them clamoring to help."

"What did you expect? Did you see those reporters out there? Did you think about the tour or label before doing what you did?" Anger bubbling over, Zander crossed his arms over his chest. "You're a fucking moron."

"A moron? I guess you haven't made any mistakes?" Luke's tone rose. He got right in Zander's space.

"Not like this," he murmured. His hands formed fists with the urge to knock that sneer off Luke's face.

They were nose-to-nose when Irisa pushed in between them. "Not here. Are you insane?"

Luke's lawyer grabbed his client's shoulder and pulled him away. "We're going outside. No matter what anyone says to you, don't engage, don't respond. Let me handle it."

After nodding at him, Irisa kept her hand on Zander's chest. "We're all leaving. You're all going to pretend nothing is wrong, and then you're going to get in the car."

Nothing wrong? The laugh fell from his lips. "Sure. United front. No problems here."

"That's right. Now move it. Fast."

Zander kept his gaze straight ahead and ignored the questions thrown at him while Luke's lawyer handled the media. Luke had gotten off easy. He should be grateful his band mate wouldn't be doing jail time, but all he wanted to do was break away from the media circus before he ended up hitting someone.

When they reached the parking lot, Irisa pulled up short. "I need to make a call."

He'd seen Oliver's name and several missed calls on her phone. Funneling his anger at Oliver into his frustration with Luke, Zander leaned against his sister's car, aware of the reporters and cameras. "Maybe we should make this leg of the tour a dry one."

"No alcohol?" Landry shook his head. "Are you serious?"

Luke loosened his tie. "No fucking way. What about our brewery sponsorship, genius? It's pretty hard for us to promote it if we can't drink it. Wait, unless you meant the dry tour for just me. And if so, that's not happening."

Brendan stepped between them. "Come on, guys. Calm down."

"A dry tour," Landry muttered. "What're you thinking we drink instead—milk and cookies?"

"Dude." Brendan looked at him, expression serious, and tone of voice to match. "You can't drink cookies."

Zander groaned and shook his head. Landry cracked a smile and even Luke huffed out a laugh, which grew louder as Brendan laughed at his own joke. The tension eased, and for a moment everything negative and stressful faded, leaving only the warm sunshine spotlighting the friends he'd had for more than a decade. But then Luke's lawyer coughed, and reality returned. The courthouse, the cameras across the parking lot, their responsibilities, the mounting frustrations, and the knowledge that

no matter how much he wanted things to be perfect,
he couldn't have it all.

CHAPTER THREE

Later that afternoon, Jayne headed into the animal shelter, music playing in her ears, the melodies working their soothing magic on her spirits. She'd been volunteering there for years and it had become a home away from home. The first few times back after Pepper's death had been hard. She'd dealt with the pain by listening to music, her go-to solution for any problem. Two months later, it still wasn't easy, but today, she'd have Irisa for company, if her friend wasn't held up too long in court. They scheduled their volunteer hours together whenever they could.

"Jayne." Irisa's voice came from behind her.

Jayne turned, pulling her earbuds out of her ears. Waiting all day for word on Luke had left her edgy. Heck, she'd been a bit on edge from the moment she'd first met him. "Hi. How's everything with Luke?"

Irisa smiled. "Good news—the tour will go on as planned."

Dread deflated to a dull ache. She should be happy—it was a good paying job. But part of her had hoped for not so happy news. She'd hate to see the band have to cancel their tour, but after the icy reception she'd received, spending time with the bickering bunch wasn't very appealing. Jayne stopped walking. She took a deep breath and said the thing that had been on her mind all weekend. "I don't think he likes me."

"Of course he likes you." Irisa waved off the comment. "The band's been having some issues, that's all. He was in an equally bad mood with everyone on Friday. He's really a nice guy, though. I promise."

"I don't know." Wringing her hands together, she glanced at the ground. "I've dealt with high-drama bands before. It doesn't scare me, but it's also never been directed *at* me. I don't want to leave you stranded but I'm not sure I'm the best choice for this band."

Irisa reached into her pocket and pulled out a roll of antacids. She popped a pink tablet free. "I'll give you more money."

"Money isn't the issue. You're already paying me more than I expected."

"I promise things will be fine. Please don't back out. I need you."

Jayne studied the roll as Irisa pocketed it again. "How many of those have you taken today? You're chewing them every time I see you. Are you sick?"

"No." Her answer too quick, she chewed the tablet. "What can I do to convince you to come on tour?"

"Are you sure you're all right?" The last thing she needed was to worry about her friend. Irisa was more than a friend, more like a sister.

"I'd feel better if I knew you were still coming with me."

"Well…" Backing out of something after she'd given her word wasn't her style. But she was emotionally exhausted after Pepper's ordeal, and she did have Vendetta's tour coming up in July. The high-energy metal band was very high-maintenance.

Irisa gripped her hands together. "Being the only girl stinks. When we were playing the shows in New York and New Jersey, I spent a lot of time with the fashion designer who outfitted the guys for their photo shoot in Central Park. Hanging out with Audrey made me realize how much fun it was to have another female around. Please come help balance out all that testosterone."

Her friend had mentioned Audrey Pierce's name several times when they'd spoken during that tour. Obviously, the designer had made an impact. Jayne touched her gold pendant—an Audrey Pierce design.

Irisa had also flown home during that tour to hold Jayne's hand as she said goodbye to Pepper, and then spent the next three days helping her deal with the void the dog's death had left. She could never repay the debt. "I can't say no to you. All right. I'm in. I'm no quitter."

A grin overtook Irisa's face and she threw her arms around Jayne. "Thank you."

Arm in arm, they walked into the puppy room. Cute bundles of fur yipped and played and vied for attention. Jayne groomed and snuggled and let them soothe her worries. She'd been through a lot in her life. She could handle one surly singer.

Confidence restored, she turned to find Irisa playing with a German Shepherd. "Do you want to grab drinks later? I have to give two piano lessons first, but maybe around eight?"

"I was thinking I'd stay home tonight." A blush colored her cheeks. "I'm hoping I'll bump into my new neighbor again. We sort of had drinks together on Friday night."

"Sort of had drinks together?" Jayne set aside the brush she held. "How could you not tell me?"

"The whole Luke situation kind of dominated my thoughts."

"True." She didn't want to dwell on that anymore. Irisa had been alone for far too long. If anyone needed to have some fun, she did. "Come on, spill the details."

"Well, his name is Dom Torres and he plays center field for the Riptide. He also happens to be a big fan of the band. He even uses "Cut Down" as his walk-up song."

"Wow. I bet the guys love that."

"They do. They're performing the National Anthem at the ball park on the seventeenth and they'll get to meet the team afterward. Zander can't wait."

"How's he doing?" Jayne picked up her brush, hoping the casual movement would cover her interest. She could only imagine the band's response to Luke's boating-under-the-influence arrest.

"You actually might hear from him. He asked me for your number today. I think he's worried you might bail out." She stared out the window for a moment, a frown marring her forehead. "You won't, right?"

"I already said I was in." She couldn't prevent

the edge from seeping into her voice. Would Zander really care if she came on the tour? With all he had going on and pulling his focus, she doubted she was at the forefront of his thoughts.

A few hours later, she strode into the community center in south L.A., where she gave piano lessons once a week. The building, a source of renewal in the crumbling neighborhood, had seen better days. Kids of all ages ran across the tiled floor, spilling into various rooms. She waved to some of the regulars and made her way to the music room. Instruments, some in various need of repair, crowded the space. Because the center relied on volunteers to provide free music lessons to the kids, they often went for long periods without instructors, and the instruments came in by way of donations. Most of the kids couldn't afford to buy their own. Their families could barely afford clothing and food.

After her beginner lesson with a six-year-old more interested in banging on the keys than learning scales, she hunted down the director. She found Kate in one of the common areas.

"Got a minute?"

Kate grinned and blew out a breath. "For you? Always."

"I'm taking a job with The Fury for eight weeks." Jayne handed her a list of dates. "There are a few conflicts with the piano lessons. I'd like to see if we can reschedule them rather than cancel them."

"You're touring with The Fury?" A young, familiar voice came from behind her.

She turned. Dalton, one of the kids in the program, stood gaping at her. As usual, he wore a threadbare concert t-shirt advertising one of The Fury's tours. He always talked about the band and how he wanted to play the guitar like Zander one day.

"Have you already met them? What're they like? Does Zander really bring his guitar everywhere he goes?" Excitement shined in his eyes.

"Yes, interesting, and no." She smiled. "How are the guitar lessons?"

The shine faded. "The teacher quit. He said he didn't feel safe coming here."

"I'm sorry."

"Yeah, well. Maybe someone else will want to do it." Thin shoulders hunched forward. "But nothing's going good for me lately, so I'm not holding my breath."

One of the other kids yelled for him to join in a basketball game. He declined until Kate managed to convince him he was needed. When he left, Kate sighed. "I feel so bad for him. His parents are going through a bitter divorce. He hasn't smiled in weeks, and he's shutting himself off from his friends. The only thing that seemed to make him happy was those guitar lessons. He looks so defeated."

"I know just how he feels." Jayne could sympathize all too well. Divorce was usually harder on the kids. "Since I'm working with the band, maybe I can arrange for Dalton to meet them. At least Zander, since he's his favorite."

"Could you? That would mean so much to him.

Dalton's such a special kid."

He was. Shy and sweet, with a desperation she recognized. The idea warmed her spirit, and hopefully Zander would agree. Volunteering was important to Irisa, and from what she knew of Zander, giving back was important to him too. "I'll call him now."

He answered on the second ring. "Hello."

"It's Jayne." Her heart pounded in her chest.

"I know." His voice warmed and the words slid over her skin. "So…what's going on?"

She twisted her necklace chain around her fingers. After all the drama, meeting with another fan might be the last thing he wanted to do. "I need to ask a favor. But you can say no. Really, it's okay."

A low, rich laugh flowed through the speaker. "How about you tell me what it is first?"

"I volunteer at a community center in south L.A. One of the students in the music program idolizes you. He's sixteen, his parents are divorcing, and he's been going through a really rough time lately. He only wears Fury concert t-shirts and is always talking about how you're his favorite guitarist." She paused and drew in a breath. "It would be a huge boost for him to meet you. Do you think you could meet with him?"

"Well—"

"I realize we just met and I know you're exhausted from the tour. But he's got virtually no one. He reminds me so much of me when I was his age. My parents suffered an ugly divorce, too. I know it would mean a lot to him."

"Jayne." He laughed again. "It's okay. I'll do it."

"Really?"

"Sure. When is a good time?"

"He's here now. And he's usually here most afternoons. I'm sure he could be here whenever you can schedule it."

"So you're both there now?"

"Yes."

"Why wait? Text me the address and I'll head over."

"*Now?*" Glancing down at her t-shirt, worn jeans, and sneakers, she winced. But this meeting was for Dalton, not her. "That should be fine."

"I'll see you soon." His voice deepened and her knees turned to jelly.

She stared at the phone. "Kate, he's on his way."

"Exciting," Kate rubbed her hands together like an evil genius plotting a takeover. "Let's keep this a surprise. I'll stay with Dalton and watch the game. You wait by the front desk."

Too soon, she spied Zander cutting across the parking lot. He met her gaze through the glass front door and quickened his pace. Leather jacket, dark jeans, black shirt, he caught the attention of every person in the room.

She ignored the urge to straighten her shirt or touch her hair. "Thank you for coming."

His gaze roamed her from head to toe. "This is much better than how I was spending my evening."

"What were you doing?"

"Hanging out with Shredder."

"Shredder?"

"My dog. You'll meet him soon." He glanced around the room. "I haven't been in a place like this in years. Looks just like the one I hung out in. Actually, this isn't all that far from where I grew up."

She knew his story from Irisa. His family had emigrated from the Ukraine when he and Irisa were little kids. They hadn't had much money. In this space, he didn't look like a big-time rock star, just a regular guy. "Dalton's playing basketball. We didn't tell him you were coming." She led the way.

After introducing Zander to Kate, she pointed out Dalton.

Zander nodded and waited for a break in play. Then he walked over and tapped Dalton's shoulder. "Got a minute?"

The teen whirled around. His eyes grew rounder and rounder. "You're…you're…"

"Zander Rostov." Grinning, he extended his hand. "And you're Dalton, right?"

"Yeah. How are you actually here? Is this for real?" He slowly raised his hand to shake Zander's when the rocker pulled him in for a quick, back-slapping hug.

Zander handed Dalton a new concert t-shirt. "I hear you play the guitar."

Jayne relaxed against the wall and watched as Dalton bloomed into full animation as he discussed music with his idol.

After several minutes, Dalton led Zander into the music room and Jayne followed to spy from a distance. Dalton showed Zander the guitar he'd been using. "I've been playing for two years. I'm trying to learn your solo in "My Fist, Your Face"."

"Show me what you've got." Zander stood back and observed, then gave pointers. They worked together for a while, far longer than she'd expected.

Dalton beamed. "This is great. Unreal. I can't believe you're teaching me how to play your song."

"You're doing a good job. Keep it up."

"I'll try. I'll be doing it on my own, though. My teacher quit this week."

Jayne cleared her throat, drawing the attention of both males. "Kate's already posted a notice. I'm sure we'll have a new volunteer soon."

A frown marred Zander's forehead. Worry that he'd think she was trying to coerce him into working with Dalton tightened her stomach. He cocked his head to the side and studied the guitar in Dalton's hands. "You know, some of the best guitarists are self-taught."

"Were you self-taught?" Hero-worship shined in Dalton's eyes.

"Some, but I also had a teacher, one of the best. He passed away a few years ago." Zander crouched beside his chair. "Maybe we can get together here sometimes to jam."

"Really? You'd do that?"

"Sure, man. You have a natural talent and a good ear. I can't have you not playing."

Dalton's chest puffed up. He swung his gaze to Jayne. "Wow. Did you hear that?"

"That's incredibly generous." She let her gaze roam over Zander. Calm features, relaxed stance, no signs of resentment.

He winked at her and then turned back to

Dalton. "We're doing a show at The Caboose on Saturday. Want to come? You can hang around and help my guitar tech. Chad's a good guy. He'd get a kick out of having you there."

"Yeah. That would be awesome."

Shaking her head, Jayne moved toward them. "I know some shows there are eighteen-and-over, but he's only sixteen." When Dalton winced at her words, she smiled through a stab of sympathy. Embarrassing him hadn't been her intention. But if he arrived and they wouldn't let him in…

Zander waved away her concern. "I've known Jake, the owner, for years. He'll be fine with it because Dalton will be with us. Just get permission from your parents."

"All they do is fight with each other. They don't know or care if I'm home or not." The forlorn, lost-puppy look was back.

"Give me your number. I'll call to clear it with them." He waited while the teen rattled off a number and his parents' names. To her surprise, he made the call right there. Within minutes, he'd obtained permission from Dalton's mother, assured her he'd arrange for her son's transportation to and from the show, promised her someone from the center would accompany him, and then convinced an ecstatic Dalton to rejoin his friends in their basketball game.

Once they were alone, Zander leaned in and lowered his voice. "The kid wasn't kidding. His parents were fighting when his mom answered the phone."

"That breaks my heart. He's been so unhappy

lately but what you're doing made his day. You're really going all-out for a kid you just met." An awful thought entered her mind. "I hope you don't think I was hinting around at anything when I mentioned the volunteer thing."

"Believe it or not, I think I'm the one getting the better end of this deal."

"Why's that?"

"I like helping him, and I'll get to spend the night looking at you."

Warmth crept into her cheeks. "Looking at me?"

"Oh yeah. And don't pretend you don't know you're totally stunning. And each time I see you, I find even more things that I like." His fingers trailed a teasing path over the back of her hand, scrambling her thoughts. "So for Saturday, the show's at nine. Can you get there at eight-thirty? We'll meet at the side entrance in the parking lot and all go in together."

"I don't want to be a distraction." She twisted her necklace around her fingers and grasped the pendant in her hand. She couldn't afford a distraction like him.

He propped his arm against the wall and his hand brushed her shoulder. His quick smile shot heat through her. "His mom wanted Kate to be there. I want you to come too. It'll be good for Dalton to have some familiar faces."

How had he moved so close? Jayne gazed at him, and the fine lines etched into his forehead.

His hand closed over hers. "Come."

Looking in his eyes, the brown edged with

green, intense and focused on her like she was the most interesting creation he'd ever seen, she couldn't say no.

CHAPTER FOUR

Helping Dalton had infused him with fresh energy. Throughout the week, Zander jotted down tips and techniques he could teach the kid.

Jayne wasn't far from his thoughts either. She'd looked so cute at the center, like one of the kids with her old t-shirt and faded jeans. Thoughts kept him distracted during the party with the fans on Tuesday, kept him subdued enough to play nice with his band mates, and kept him calm during a press event on Thursday, when the media hounded him about Luke's arrest. He'd repeated the same canned lines about fully supporting his friend, then answered the same old tired questions the press fired out at nearly every interview: How did you guys get your start? What's your favorite band? If you were a flavor of ice cream, what would you be? He still shook his head over that last one.

Finally, Saturday rolled around. He drove down to The Caboose, one of his favorite places to play. The bar, a generic brick building with its scarred wood floors and awesome acoustics was like a second home. Jake had given The Fury their start long ago and in return would forever have their support. They attended meet-and-greets and played special performances there several times a year.

As Zander pulled in to a spot, Brendan sped into the one beside him. They walked toward the side entrance where Landry and Luke leaned against the wall.

Luke raised a brow. "Once again, you live the closest and you're the last one here."

"It's not even seven-thirty yet, so why do you care?" Zander scanned the lot for Dalton.

"Technically, *I* was last." Brendan put in. He threw his arm over Luke's shoulder. "Hey, is that the kid?"

The car service Zander hired pulled into the lot. "Yeah. Don't scare him."

Dalton got out, grin wide and wearing the new Fury t-shirt Zander had given him.

He waved, beckoning the teen to join them.

"Guys, this is Dalton. He's going to be shadowing Chad tonight." He introduced the boy to his band mates, Chad, and a few other members of the road crew. Dalton's eyes grew wider and wider with each new *hello*.

A sleek green sedan glided into the lot. Jayne, Irisa, and Kate emerged. Zander made the introduction rounds again before they finally headed inside.

Equipment set up didn't take long. He chatted with Jake while keeping watch from the side of the stage. Had it been almost ten years since that first time they'd played at the bar, with only a handful of people lounged at the tables? Tonight, the crowd packed in, around tables, and three-deep at the front of the stage. It was unreal. As always, gratitude overwhelmed him.

In the corner of his vision, Jayne approached. In navy jeans and a blue tank top sprinkled with glitter, she resembled a mermaid emerging from the sea. His groin tightened and he gripped his guitar so hard the strings bit into his callouses. Forcing himself to relax, he set it aside. "Hey."

Jayne's gaze swept over him, from his hands to his face. "Do you need anything?"

Those curves and those lips wrapped around him would be a good place to start. But he had a show to put on and didn't want the one hundred people surrounding them watching their first kiss. "I'm good, thanks. You're not here to work tonight. Relax and have a good time."

She glanced at the screaming crowd. "They're more than ready for you to play."

"So am I." But rather than plucking his guitar strings, his fingers itched to play across her skin. He needed to distract himself from those thoughts. "Dalton's a good kid." The teen stood with Chad, nodding over something the tech said.

"He really is. Thank you for letting him do this. He'll never forget it."

He shrugged off her thanks with a wave of his hand. "It's nice to feel needed." Better than nice.

Under the house lights, her hair appeared more coppery red than her regular rose-gold, reminding him of the sky at sunset. He couldn't resist temptation and slid a strand between his fingers to see if it felt as warm as the hue hinted.

Eyes darkened, she watched his hand slide off the end of her hair. "I know what you mean. That's how I feel when I'm doing my job too."

Luke stomped past them, grumbling about something under his breath. Two crew members followed. Jayne shifted into him and out of their path, and Zander held still to resist locking his hands around her waist and drawing her against him. He settled for resting his hand on her shoulder. The warmth of her skin only teased him. Her perfume drifted around them, a sultry cloak separating them from the rest of the world.

Jake stepped onstage. "Are you guys ready?"

Zander glanced around him. Brendan, Landry, and Luke were already in position. "Let's do it."

"Break a leg." Jayne's fingers drifted across his.

He blew out a breath as she sauntered away. Jake's brief introduction allowed him a minute to switch gears. Blood humming, he played the opening riff of "Cut Down".

The crowd went wild, shifting from cheering into singing along. After the song, he handed his blue Gibson to Chad. For over eight years, no one had touched his guitars but Chad or him, but Dalton was right there—with Zander's red Fender in hand—for the switch. The kid must have impressed his tech. He nodded his thanks and Dalton grinned. Brendan's crashing drums launched the next song, and Zander shredded, playing the intro solo with lightning speed, to the fans' cheers and chanting that lasted through their eight song set.

Shows at the bar used to end with tossing back drinks with the fans. But tonight was different. Jayne's presence was enough to spike his blood. She outshined everyone else in the room. He still signed autographs and posed for pictures, all the while keeping an eye on Dalton. He couldn't help hoping Jayne would hang around long enough for him to say goodnight.

Dalton buzzed around from band member to band member, asking questions. Having the kid around kept them on pretty decent behavior with each other. He was impressed by Dalton's willingness to help out with anything the crew needed. After the chaos wound down, he joined him in front of his rack of guitars. "You said you don't have a guitar at home, right?"

"Right."

He gestured to the rack. "Pick any one of them, except the blue one."

"You're giving me one of *your* guitars?"

"You need something so you can practice. You'll need an amp too. Talk to Chad. He'll hook you up."

"Man, this is unreal." Dalton gazed at the guitars. He reached for the red Fender. "Maybe someday I'll be able to play "Temperature Rising" as good as you."

Zander felt like Santa at Christmas. The band donated items frequently, but this up close, first-hand experience of seeing the happiness on Dalton's face was, in the kid's words, unreal.

Turning, he caught Jayne watching the exchange and smiling. The warmth flowing through him headed south. He wasn't helping the kid to impress her. But if that happened, it would be a nice side benefit because he fully intended to get to know her on a much more personal level.

***

Jayne arrived at the gates of Zander's large Spanish-style home, but before she could roll down her window to touch the speaker button, they swung open. She followed the winding drive and parked beside Irisa's blue BMW. The nerves churning her stomach increased. Zander's invitation for Jayne to watch the band practice and to attend the next day's ball game had seemed like a good idea, until now. He'd been too tempting at the community center and at the show—all caring and sweet under that sexy exterior. Nearly a week had passed since that night at The Caboose. Since the show, she'd reminded herself that getting involved with a client wasn't a smart idea. But then she'd remember something he'd said, or the way he'd looked at her, and forget all about why mixing business and pleasure was a bad idea, and she'd be back to square one.

Before she could knock, the front door opened wide. Zander stood in the threshold, hair disheveled, and wearing a black t-shirt that pulled tight across his broad shoulders. A sexy smile slowly spread across his face. "Hey. You made it."

"I hope I'm not late." She brushed her hand through her hair. The drive had taken a little longer than she'd anticipated.

"We didn't start yet. Luke and Brendan aren't here." He stepped back and gestured to the large room at his back. "Come in."

She stepped into the foyer. Coffee scented the air. He gave her the nickel tour, just long enough for her to appreciate the Spanish motif—smooth archways, high vaulted ceilings, hardwood floors with a few well-placed fireplaces. The large kitchen opened out to a slate patio and pool. They breezed by the generous living room and she stole a quick peek at the game room, dominated by an elaborate pool table, before they entered the studio used for practice. Landry and Irisa called out greetings when she walked in. Guitars, a drum kit, and various sized amps spread across the room. A couch and two chairs lined one of the walls under framed photos of the band and several rock legends.

The pictures normally would draw her interest but the large English Bulldog on the floor captured her attention. He lifted his head and regarded her, then staggered to his paws.

Landry laughed. "Whoa, Shredder's deemed Jayne worthy enough for a proper greeting. He must like you."

"He usually needs a lot of motivation to move." Zander crouched beside his dog. "You can pet him, it's okay."

She knelt beside Zander, her knee pressing into the side of his thigh. Shredder lumbered closer and dropped his head into her lap. Zander's fingers brushed over hers as the both scratched the dog's head. Each time their fingers touched, electricity sparked up her arm.

When the doorbell rang, he pulled away with a sigh. He left the room and returned a minute later with Luke and Brendan.

Luke scowled at her and Irisa. "What are you guys doing here?"

Irisa laughed. "Hello to you, too. I thought it

would be fun for us to sit in."

The temperature in the room seemed to drop with his icy stare. Jayne joined Irisa on the couch. Shredder looked up from his spot on the floor and gave a low grumble before following to settle at her feet.

"I think Shredder's found someone he likes more than his owner." Brendan took a gummy bear out of the container by the drum kit and popped it in his mouth.

"Can you blame him?" Zander picked up an acoustic guitar from a stand near the wall. "Before we practice the anthem, here's something I've been playing with."

His fingers strummed the strings. The melody pulled her in, pulled at something inside her, and filled a yearning she didn't even know she had. Zander's fingers on the guitar, his expression, the concentration, drew her in as much as the music. When the last note faded, he looked up for the first time since he started played and stared right into her eyes. For a moment, she thought he could see into her soul.

"You want to add that in the set list?" Luke's curt voice cut in, a sharp contrast to the romantic song. "We don't have anything else like it."

"I think our fans could handle us giving them something in a different direction." He began playing it again.

"Are you writing lyrics or leaving it instrumental?" Landry began picking out notes on his bass while Brendan softly tapped the high hat to the beat.

Again, Zander's gaze tracked to Jayne. "It's pretty new, so I'm not sure yet."

She offered him a smile and her honest opinion. "I thought it was beautiful."

"Yeah?" His grin spread across his face.

Luke shook his head. "We aren't some soft ballad band, man."

"It's *one* song." With a shrug, Zander adjusted the strap on his guitar. "You don't need to worry about it because you're not singing this one anyway."

The singer crossed his arms over his chest. "Let me guess, you are?"

"Come on, guys. We have company here. We can settle this later." Irisa's forced cheerfulness fell flat amid air thick with tension. Luke continued glaring at Zander, and Zander scowled back.

Two gummy bears arced through the air, one hitting Luke's chest and one landing on Zander's head.

"Damn it, Brendan." Zander picked the red gummy out of his hair. "Dude, if that had gone into my guitar…"

"Relax. My aim's not that good…yet." Eyes dancing with laughter, he twirled his drumsticks.

"I can't work in these fucking conditions," Luke grumbled, but his tone lost a lot of heat.

Irisa leaned toward her. "I forgot to mention the bears…"

When Brendan shrugged, all innocence, Jayne couldn't help cracking a smile. He tossed another gummy into the air and caught it in his mouth. "Want one?"

"Thanks, but I think I'll let you keep your stockpile."

Zander winged the red gummy back at the drummer, but he grinned when he threw it, and then he focused those hazel eyes on Jayne. "Did you know Shredder can sing and play the drums?"

"Can he?" She shared his smile. He looked so good when he smiled... "I'd love to see that."

He nodded and called the dog over to Brendan's kit, then knelt and positioned the dog's back leg by the base drum. "Okay, boy. Sing."

He strummed a few notes and Shredder let out a few barks and yips, followed by a howl. His back leg and his tail thumped the drum. The sounds mixed in with Zander's playing and didn't sound too bad. Every time he pointed to the dog, Shredder would let out a single bark.

Jayne laughed. "You should take him on the road with you."

Landry set down his bass. "We have. Where do you think he learned to do this? Hours and hours, driving across the country."

"Now that we're finished goofing off, can we get back to work?" Luke stood in the middle of the room, hands splayed on his hips. The brooding scowl once again darkened his features.

Zander exchanged the acoustic guitar for his blue Gibson. "What's your deal, man?"

"Maybe I have something else to do."

Did they have to argue? Jayne shifted in her seat. After growing up in a house filled with fighting and tension, she avoided it at all costs. When Luke spun in her direction, her first thought was to soothe. Maybe he was angry about his forced driving ban. "If you need to go somewhere, I can drive you."

"I'll grab a cab." He paused and thought for a moment. "Later."

Shredder padded over and lay over her feet. Leaning down, she scratched his head, absorbing comfort, and then slid to the floor and rubbed his belly, giving him her undivided attention while the guys ran through the National Anthem close to a dozen times. No drums for the ballpark. Brendan harmonized with Luke while Zander and Landry played the melody.

Finally, the guys were satisfied. Either that or they were tired of each other or of playing the same song so many times. Luke and Irisa left first. He'd accepted a ride home from her. While Landry chatted with Zander, Brendan sat beside Jayne. "For the tour, can you make sure I have gummy bears at every show?"

She smiled. "For eating or for launching attacks on your band mates?"

"Both." He shrugged. "Things can get pretty heated and it lowers the tension."

She'd witnessed that first-hand. "Don't worry, I've got you covered."

"Thanks. I'll see you tomorrow at the ballpark." He stood and said his goodbyes to Zander and Landry. When all three men walked toward the doorway, Jayne got to her feet. As much as she loved playing with the dog, she didn't want to overstay her welcome.

Zander turned back. "You don't have to go. He

hasn't had this much attention in a while."

Shredder barked and nudged his head against her legs. Zander laughed, and the rich sound echoed through the room and sent a flutter of awareness through her blood. "See? He's asking you to stay."

"All right." Her heart beat faster. She bent down and rubbed the dog's head. "It's pretty tough to say goodbye to you. We can play a little longer."

Zander rewarded her with a smile before following the guys out of the room. She rejoined Shredder on the floor and tried not to dwell on the fact that she was now alone with the one man who tempted her to throw caution and rules out the window.

***

Zander closed the door behind his band mates and made his way back into the practice room. Jayne sprawled on the floor playing with the dog. Her hair fell over her shoulders and a smile as brilliant as a sunbeam lighted her face.

"Looks like he made a new friend."

She smiled. "I love dogs. I was the kid who always brought home strays."

He knew she volunteered at the animal shelter with his sister. "Do you have any pets?"

"I had Pepper, my Yorkie, for six years. She passed away two months ago." A shadow clouded her eyes.

Shit. He joined her on the floor, and mirrored her position, back against the couch, forearms resting on his knees. "I'm sorry. Losing a pet is like losing a family member."

"It's true. Especially with Pepper. I adopted her when she was eight weeks old. We went through a lot together. She was the runt of the litter, and had all sorts of health problems from the beginning. But the last eighteen months, she battled cancer."

"I'm so sorry." He remembered Irisa flying home during their East Coast tour to visit Jayne. And now he remembered why.

"I tried every type of treatment to save her, but it wasn't enough." Her voice quavered. She cleared her throat and cuddled closer to Shredder. "But I'm happy she's not in pain anymore."

Shredder nudged his head into her legs again. Comfort offered, canine-style. Jayne's hand rubbed over his head, then she leaned over and hugged the dog. "He's a sweetie."

Zander agreed. His dog was awesome, but he needed to lighten the moment. "You know, his master's pretty good too."

At that, her head came up. "Yeah?"

"Sure. Once you get to know him." He shifted closer. Her breath caught when his elbow brushed against the side of her breast. The little hitch of breath aroused him immediately.

Her eyes deepened to darker shades of blue. "I like what I know so far."

"Do you? Me, too." He leaned down until only a few inches separated them and trailed his fingertip down her cheek and across her mouth. He'd been dreaming of tasting her lips for days.

Those full lips parted and the look in her eyes, surprise mixed with need, sent his desire soaring.

"It's not a good idea."

"What isn't?" He could barely hear over the buzzing in his head.

"Kissing. I never get involved with someone I'm working with."

Her words and definitive tone registered loud and clear. He sat back. "I never have either." If things headed south, they'd still have to see each every day. He liked Jayne—admired her as a person. She wasn't the kind of person for a casual fling. She was also Irisa's best friend. He definitely didn't want to hurt her.

Pink spots appeared in her cheeks and her gaze dropped to Shredder. She tucked her hair behind her ear and then her fingers tangled around the gold necklace she wore. "So…"

He didn't want her to be uncomfortable. Kissing or no kissing, he liked her and wanted to get to know her better. He tapped her hand with his finger and smiled when she looked at him. "So. How'd a nice piano-playing girl like you end up being a tour manager for rock bands?"

"Music saved me. It was my escape." She shifted her position, stretching her long legs out in front of her. "I mentioned before that my parents' divorce was similar to what Dalton is going through. They had awful fights for years. I'd hide in my bedroom blaring the music as loud as I dared to drown them out. I fell in love with rock because the drums and guitars covered their arguments better than anything else."

Zander moved Shredder's bulk off of Jayne's legs. He settled the dog between them. "I gravitated to it because it's powerful and aggressive and I like playing loud."

"I noticed you tend to play the blue guitar more than any of the others you have. What makes it special?"

"I've had it the longest. I bought it when the band was just starting out, after we'd all found each other. I met Luke in college. I was studying music. He was a chemistry major. We were both in other bands that didn't work out. He knew Landry, and the three of us started hanging out, jamming, and realized we had something special. Landry met Brendan through another band, and then he joined us too. He clicked. It all fit. We all fit." He smirked. "You'd never know it from the way we've been acting lately. Anyway…"

"Anyway, it's a beautiful guitar."

"It matches your eyes. That was one of the first things I noticed about you. That, and the way your presence lights up a room." What the hell was he doing? She'd just said she didn't get involved with anyone she worked with. But he couldn't shake the chemistry between them.

Those blue eyes focused on his mouth long enough for him to consider leaning in and tasting her, consequences be damned. Her lips parted but then her gaze flicked to his eyes. "I should probably get going."

"You can stay."

"I don't think staring temptation in the face is a smart idea."

He grinned. "Maybe not, but it's a beautiful view from where I'm sitting."

The blush crept up her neck and over her cheeks. "Thank you. And on that note, I'll say goodnight."

As they stood, Shredder whined and rubbed his head against Jayne's shin. "I think he's protesting. You'll have to come back and visit him."

She gave the dog one last rub. "I don't think I could stay away."

Zander led her to the door. He'd spent so much time picturing kissing Jayne that he couldn't not see it every time he closed his eyes. Her position on not getting involved made sense, as much as he didn't want to admit it. A sadistic part of him demanded he test them both. When they reached his door, he stopped her by laying a single fingertip on her shoulder. "What, no hug goodbye?"

She clasped the gold pendant dangling from the long chain around her neck. "All right."

They opened their arms at the same time. Jayne took a step toward him and his hands closed over her shoulders and drew her into his embrace. Her curves fit against him perfectly, like they were two puzzle pieces. Soft golden-red hair brushed his cheek and he inhaled the scent of honeysuckle. She'd turned her face toward his chest rather than away and when he looked down, her eyes were closed. Her chest rose and fell in time with his as she relaxed, her muscles growing soft, yielding to his form.

All he had to do was slide his hand into her hair and direct her mouth to his. His hands flexed on her back but he didn't move them further.

Releasing her was torture but he'd scored a

small victory—he'd seen how much of an effort it had cost Jayne to pull away.

CHAPTER FIVE

One of his earliest and favorite memories of his childhood was coming to the Riptide's ballpark with his dad. If someone had told him back then that one day he'd be on their field playing the National Anthem with his rock band, he'd never have believed it in a million years. Yet here he was.

Zander turned in a slow circle, taking in the scoreboard, the dugouts, the baseball diamond, the scents of grass and dirt and ballpark foods, and the murmurs from the sea of people filling the stadium's seats. Beside him, Landry and Brendan chatted with one of the security guards. Luke stood off to the side performing the series of breathing exercises he did before every show. He'd been quiet on the ride to the stadium, sitting in the back of the SUV Irisa had hired to drive them, scowling and saying nothing.

Irisa and Jayne would be watching from one of the suites. Keeping his mind off of Jayne and the way she'd felt in his arms hadn't worked. She didn't get involved with people she worked with, he didn't either, and the band typically hired the same people over and over again. Irisa seemed happier with Jayne on tour. He wouldn't be surprised if Irisa wanted her again for the next one. Pursuing Jayne wouldn't be smart. But they could be friends. With maybe some harmless flirting added in.

The crowd cheered as the two teams filed onto the field and stood in front of their respective dugouts.

Show time.

A rush of energy flooded his body. Zander glanced at the band. "Let's rock this place."

He played the opening strains of the anthem and it rang out from the stadium's giant speakers. Landry's bass followed, his accompaniment filling out the low end of the song. He grinned. This was so fucking cool.

Luke grabbed hold of the mic and belted out the lyrics, his voice strong, his pitch perfect. Brendan joined in. Not having his drums didn't stop his fingers from moving. They tapped the side of his leg, keeping time with the music.

Too soon, the last chords faded. Luke thanked the fans and rallied the crowd for a Riptide win. Flying high, Zander led the way to the line of Riptide players. He went down the line, receiving either handshakes or high fives. Dom Torres, one of his favorite players, stood at the end. He had an inkling that his sister's sudden interest in baseball stemmed from the center fielder's recent move into her apartment building.

He shook Dom's hand. "Good luck today."

"Thanks, man. Nice job out there. I'll see you in the locker room after the game, right?"

"I'll be there." And he'd be sure to let the ballplayer know that he had better take care of his sister.

When he reached the tunnel, he turned around for one last look, and watched the players take the field. Temptation to stay and soak in the moment battled with the temptation to get to the suite and see Jayne. Being with her was sweet torture. The one woman he wanted—and he couldn't have her.

***

After the band left the field, Jayne left her position by the window. During the performance, her gaze had been riveted to Zander's jacked frame, the way he held his guitar and the way his jeans and black t-shirt showed off well-developed muscles. Muscles she'd experienced to be as strong as they looked. Wrapped in his arms yesterday, leaning against his chest, she'd wanted nothing more than to raise her lips to his. But she never broke her own rule and got involved with any client. She excused herself and headed into the restroom. A few minutes to compose herself, to gain control of her breathing, and she would be fine.

Over the exhaust fan's noise, male voices called out—the band congratulating each other on a job well done. With one final glance at her reflection, she opened the door and stepped into the room, and came face-to-face with Luke. His smile faded and his blue eyes hardened. Without a word, he turned away. Her stomach lurched and she stood rooted to her spot as members of the road crew entered the suite and swarmed the food table.

Zander came toward her, holding two beers. "I saved you a seat."

His smile warmed the ice out of her bones. "Nice job out there."

"Thanks." His grin formed fast and he passed her a bottle. Then he guided her to a seat in the suite's first row. They had an unobstructed view of the field. She sank into the cushion and let the beer soothe her dry throat. He settled beside her, hot and tempting. His knee rested against hers and his arm brushed hers on the shared armrest. She didn't want to pull away.

"Hey." Zander's voice rumbled low.

She looked up from the bottle and her breath caught at the intensity of his gaze. He shifted closer and her pulse thudded, but before he could say anything, Brendan dropped into the seat on her other side, carrying a beer and a plate piled high with a burger and a small mountain of fries. She angled her body closer to Zander to give Brendan more room.

"Dude. Look at the Jumbotron." He pointed to a section on the other side of the field. A group of young women in one of the nosebleed sections were all wearing *I love Zander* t-shirts. They saw themselves on camera and began cheering and waving.

"Cool." Zander reached over her and snagged a fry from Brendan's plate. "Maybe I'll send them some pizzas."

The camera zoomed in on an attractive brunette pointing to the text stretched across her ample chest and the stadium filled with catcalls. She then held up a *Marry Me Zander* sign with a phone number scrawled underneath.

Jayne pulled away so her body no longer touched his. Her imagination didn't have any trouble picturing the curvy olive-skinned woman draped all over him. He had women hitting on him all the time. It wasn't his fault. He was attractive, talented, famous, and nice to the fans. Sipping her beer, she kept her focus on the ball field and away from the giant screen. Commercial break over, the play resumed.

Zander leaned in, close enough for his lips to brush her ear. "Groupies aren't my style. Neither are college-aged girls, or brunettes who broadcast their numbers on national television."

The murmured words feathered over her neck and goosebumps dotted her arms. She glanced at Brendan, but he was deep in conversation with Landry. Her gaze darted back to Zander and his intense hazel stare. "It's not my business."

His large hand touched the back of hers. "I have a thing for strawberry blonde tour managers." He spoke the words evenly, and his chin jutted in the same stubborn way that Irisa's did whenever she was adamant about something.

"Zander." She licked lips gone dry.

His gaze zeroed in on her mouth and he draped his arm over the back of her chair. Not touching her, but still there. So near she could feel his heat. He leaned in again.

The familiar guitar riff from "Cut Down" blared over the stadium. The suite erupted in cheers so loud they matched the crowd's noise level, and around her, the guys high-fived each other. Then the Jumbotron's camera panned from Dom Torres at home plate to their suite, landing on the band. The cheer turned into a roar.

She vaguely heard Irisa telling the guys to smile and wave. Seeing herself on camera, Jayne straightened her shoulders. Brendan thrust his half-eaten burger in her hand and jumped to his feet, fists raised high. The crowd went wild. Zander's hand curled around her shoulder. He leaned forward and waved. She didn't know what to do, so she smiled. The smile bloomed brighter when his hand tightened its hold. She shouldn't encourage him— she should move away—but the warmth seeping into her shoulder felt too good.

The camera turned back to Dom, and the excitement calmed down as the fans readied to watch his at-bat. Zander's fingers shifted back to her chair but he kept his focus on the field. The game dragged on, too long for her. Each time Dom came to bat, the camera panned to the band, and then to the group of Zander's fans. The fans at the concerts would likely act the same way. Getting jealous would be silly. She didn't have any claim over him. But she couldn't help it.

After the game, Security escorted them to meet the players. Zander stayed close but was immediately drawn into conversation with one of the ballplayers. The band dispersed. She stayed near Irisa and away from Luke. Most of the players made it a point to come by and say hello. A few were really friendly and asked her about other bands she'd worked with. One of them, Slade, was from Santa Clara, just like her.

"It's nice to meet a girl from back home." Slade

gave her a slow smile. He immediately put her at ease. "We're grabbing dinner at Lorenzo's. You should come."

"That will depend on my ride. The band drove here together."

"You can drive with me. I'm more than happy to take you home later."

Zander's arm dropped over her shoulder. "Thanks, but we'll meet you there."

Eyebrows arched, she turned toward him. He regarded Slade with friendly but cautious stare and then smiled down at her. "Ready to go?"

"Uh, sure." He acted like they were a couple, keeping his arm around her until they reached the car. His closeness made her feel strangely secure, but she pushed the sensation away. She always relied on herself. Dinner at Lorenzo's was just for fun; she didn't want Zander to read anything more into it.

Luke had begged off, catching a ride with one of the Riptide players. She was relieved she wouldn't have to deal with him on the ride to the restaurant. "Where's Irisa?"

He opened her door for her and greeted their driver. "She's grabbing a drink with Dom."

"Good. She needs to have some fun." She climbed into the back seat and Zander claimed the spot by her side. Brendan and Landry jumped in, arguing about one of the player's stats.

Once inside the restaurant, the players waved to them from a table at the back. She followed Brendan and Landry. Zander kept his hand pressed to her waist while they walked to the table. She tried to ignore the sizzle that zinged up her spine. Slade indicated she should sit next to him, so she did. The only other open chair was three seats away, and Zander scowled as he sat down.

She didn't like the way the waitress flirted with him, or the smile he gave with his order, or the way she kept thinking about his words, *I have a thing for strawberry blonde tour managers*. She tried to focus on Slade's conversation. One near-kiss with Zander didn't mean anything, and a relationship with him couldn't happen. She wasn't affected by him or their chemistry.

Yeah right. She swallowed a sip of water and couldn't comfort herself with the lie.

CHAPTER SIX

Day one of the tour travel was half over. The bus lumbered its way down I-5. Zander had spent the morning tucked into the bus's back room, arguing with Luke and tweaking the new song. Thanks to both heavy traffic and two car accidents that brought traffic to a standstill, they were two hours behind their estimated arrival time. A notepad and pen lay on the seat beside him. He'd began writing out lyrics, but nothing seemed to fit.

Strains of music flowed and the melody soothed him. The brain block could have stemmed from thinking about Jayne and the smiles she'd given Slade at dinner. He hadn't seen her in the three days since, until she'd arrived at the bus that morning. She'd seemed subdued. Hopefully, she wasn't regretting what she'd signed up for.

Knocking interrupted his musing. Jayne came in, juggling her laptop, a tray with two cups of coffee and a large take out bag.

He couldn't stop his grin. His fingers continued to pluck the keys. "Have a seat."

She placed the bag next to the notepad. "You never came out to get your lunch. Everyone else finished over an hour ago."

"I forgot it was there." When he was

composing or tweaking, music came before everything else. His single-mindedness helped the band succeed, but drove his sister and band mates crazy.

She nudged it closer. "You should eat."

"As long as you keep me company." He set the guitar aside and reached for the bag. Forgotten meals often ended poorly—cold gone warm or hot gone cold. He unwrapped the burger. "It's still warm."

"I heated it in the toaster oven. I didn't want you to have to eat a cold burger and fries." With a delicate shiver, she withdrew her own burger from the bag. At his raised brow, she grinned. "I got distracted too."

"What distracted you?" He took a bite of the juicy burger.

"Irisa asked me to take over your social media page and to monitor a few of the band's pages. She said you always forget to update yours. Do you mind if I handle that for you?"

"You can handle anything of mine you want." Watching her blush, he ate another bite. He hadn't enjoyed a meal so much in ages.

"You're giving me a lot of power with that statement." She focused her attention on her food. "I'll check in with you before I post anything. I'll mainly be sharing posts from the band's main page."

"I trust you." He glanced out the window. Warm burger and warm fries. He tried his coffee— warm too. When was the last time someone had bothered reheating something for him? He couldn't remember it ever happening before. That she'd even think to take that extra step warmed him even more than the food and drink.

She'd relaxed against the plush cushions while they ate. Her hair spilled around her shoulders like spun gold struck by firelight. She'd tucked her jeans-clad legs under her. The long-sleeved blue shirt she wore almost matched her eyes. He loved how they sparkled when she laughed and so he kept her laughing with stories of the early days on the road with the guys.

Even he couldn't help laughing about the cramped van that broke down more often than not. By the time it finally died in the middle of nowhere, it was was held together with duct tape and a couple of old guitar pics.

He moved their trash out of the way, and when he reclaimed his seat, she'd moved closer to him.

"What are you working on?"

"That song I played for you guys at practice the other day." She'd inspired him, but he wasn't ready to share that yet.

"I thought I recognized it when I walked back here. Can you play it again?"

"You really liked it?" He played the song, watching for her reaction.

Eyes dreamy, a small smile on her lips, she sighed. "It's beautiful."

So was she. His blood thrummed with the melody that had been playing in his head since he'd met her. He set his guitar aside and turned to face her once again. "I'm glad you think so."

Being just friends wasn't going to work.

He rested his arm along the back of the cushion

and his fingers brushed against her hair. Easing closer, until her knee bumped his thigh, he gave into the urge to cup her cheek. She gazed at him, head tilted to the side, for a long moment. Instinct demanded he claim her lips but he forced himself to hold still. He hadn't meant to touch her, but like a moth seeking heat, something about her pulled him, making him forget the promise he made to himself.

Jayne reached for him. Her hand rested on his knee. Her other hand traced his jawline. The soft pads of her fingers glided along his skin. He groaned at the sensation, and then they were moving together as one. Her lips parted on an inhale seconds before he slanted his mouth over hers. And groaned again. She had perfect lips for kissing— soft and full. The hand on her cheek slid into her hair. He fisted the red-gold strands like he'd dreamed of doing and directed her toward a better angle. When she sighed, he licked a path across her lips and then slipped inside. Soft strokes of her tongue on his and her fingers grazing his neck sent sensations straight to his groin.

Needing an anchor, he grasped the hand she'd placed on his knee. Their fingers locked together and he craved both the sweetness of their hands linking and the ultra-hot meeting of lips and tongue. Her hand tightened in his and she shifted her thigh so more of it rested on his leg. Getting close enough wasn't possible. He wanted to haul her into his lap or lay her down on the seat to discover more of her.

Movement and loud voices from the other side of the door broke through the haze of desire. Jayne stiffened in his arms. Breathing hard, she dropped her hand from his neck but couldn't pull away because of the tight grip he had on her hair. "We can't do this here."

He wasn't ready to let go. He'd barely gotten a taste. Landry and Brendan's voices erupted in shouts and laughter. "What are they doing out there?"

"Showing Irisa how to play some video game with lots of explosions." Up close, he could see the flecks of light blue mixed in that deep ocean color like breaking waves.

More laughter and talking echoed back, and the voices grew louder. Her gaze flicked to the door and she leaned away as much as she could. Releasing his hold on her hair, he raised their joined hands to his lips and pressed a kiss against her knuckles. "If not here, then soon."

A shaky breath tumbled from her lips, swollen from his kisses. "Maybe."

"Definitely." He brushed the faint red mark that covered her cheeks and chin. "Next time, I'll make sure I shave."

***

When they reached the hotel, Jayne helped Irisa hand out keycards. For convenience, they were staying in the same block of adjoining rooms, on a low floor per Brendan's preference, and on an even-numbered floor to suit Landry. Luke hadn't voiced any preferences, not to her, but then again, he wouldn't speak to her. And Zander kept looking at her like he couldn't wait to devour her again. She shivered, wanting that too.

But they were officially on tour business. She'd made her rule for a reason, and she didn't need anything to interfere with how well she could do her job. Zander was the biggest distraction to ever challenge her rule.

Members of the co-headlining band, Assertive Ire, trooped into the lobby. The bands were friends; Zander and their front man, Griffin, went way back. The groups meshed well together, but Assertive Ire had a reputation for being fairly destructive. Hopefully that wouldn't translate over to The Fury.

With the other band around, the guys immediately began planning things for their off hours. Jayne slipped up to her room to relax. She needed time away from Zander to think. That kiss, his hands, the way he'd held her... Her gaze kept slipping to the interior door which separated her room from his. As much as she wanted him, as much as he made her feel desired, the kiss had been a lapse in judgment. All a result of that song, which never failed to make her want things she shouldn't.

When the knock came on her interior door later that night, she pretended she was asleep. And when faint notes from the guitar slipped under the door and into her heart, she tucked in ear plugs and pretended she wasn't affected at all.

She managed to avoid him for a full day and a half by bogging herself down in tour details and double and triple checking everything she could. She begged Irisa for even more work. Her friend, initially so desperate for her to tag along on the tour, now resisted relinquishing her duties. But

Jayne persisted and soon had more work than she'd normally handle.

At opening night sound check, Jayne couldn't hide any longer. Zander's gaze kept tracking to her and she felt the intensity of his unspoken questions. She stood off to the side of the stage, watching both bands play a joint song they planned to perform that night. Loud and aggressive, the cover, a number-one hit of one of rock's classic bands, took on an extra dose of energy with the added wailing guitars, double the drums, and with both Luke and Griffin taking the vocals.

They finished and Zander headed her way but she let her attention get caught by one of the crew members. He was gone when she turned back and her stomach ached with a pang of regret.

Luke strode to her, the glowering gaze not quite as severe as usual. She gripped her pendant and pasted on a smile. He didn't cut eye contact, didn't turn away, but came right up to her. "I need tea."

She glanced around the emptying stage, searching for something to mark the occasion of him actually speaking to her. "There's black tea in the dressing room."

He shook his head. "I need licorice root tea. I always drink it before a performance."

"That wasn't on the list of items you guys gave me. Can you drink something else as a substitute today and I'll make sure you have it for tomorrow?"

"No. You'll have to go out and get it." He loomed over her, as tall as Zander, and seemed primed for a fight.

But his expression was nothing like Zander.

Zander wasn't cold and angry. Her stomach tightened in that awful way she hated. She took a breath and looked past Luke's scowl. His request wasn't that unusual. Other bands she'd worked with had made special requests. One forgotten item, one time, wasn't a big deal. "All right. I'll see if I can find it."

He didn't say anything further. One brief dip of his head, a semblance of a nod, and he was gone.

"You're welcome." Part of her job was to keep the guys happy, but maybe if he noticed she didn't mind this extra chore, he'd stop scowling and glaring at her every time their eyes met.

One of the arena's interns pointed her in the direction of a specialty grocery store a short distance away. Twenty minutes later, she presented the tea to Luke.

"Here you go, licorice root tea." She set the box on the table in the dressing room.

He muttered something she decided to interpret as *thanks*. It wasn't much, but maybe it was a start.

Zander came in. Her heartbeat thudded—fast and hard and loud. She hugged her clipboard to her chest and forced a grin. "Well, I have a lot to check on out there. See you guys later."

He frowned and his eyes narrowed, but she skirted past him and into the safety of the behind the scenes chaos, managing to keep things at a professional distance for the rest of the night.

The next show the following night, gave her a sense of déjà vu. Evading Zander, staying busy, and she pretended to be fine. She stood backstage, going over her lists, while the band decided what to do for dinner, their voices carrying from the dressing room.

"My throat lozenges aren't in the dressing room." Luke's voice, as much as his scowl, snapped her spine straight.

She checked the page of items the guys had requested. "They're not on the list."

A shrug lifted his shoulders. He didn't appear apologetic. "I guess I forgot to add them. But I need them."

She sighed. Irisa hadn't mentioned that Luke was so absentminded. But if this was what Irisa usually put up with then she'd do it too—after all, it was a temporary job. "I'll find some for you."

"Lemon or honey flavored. Leave it in the dressing room." He walked away, dismissing her without waiting for a response.

His gruff bark reminded her of the dogs in the shelter. Some rescues or strays had to be socialized all over again, and some took a long time to give their trust. Patience and gentle handling worked well for them. Maybe it would work for Luke.

"Jayne." Zander's voice rumbled low, jolting her out of her musing. He stood entirely too close and smelled entirely too good. "We decided on the diner. Are you ready?"

She couldn't sit in a booth with him, pressed close together. "Actually, I have some things to do. You guys go ahead."

His brows drew together. "All right."

He didn't look happy.

She didn't feel happy.

Maybe coming on the tour had been a mistake.

CHAPTER SEVEN

A full Saturday off, with no show that night, meant a clean break from the band. Jayne spent the entire day alone away from the hotel. She turned off her phone and went to the beach, a museum, out to dinner, and to a movie. Darkness had fallen by the time she returned to the hotel.

Music came from Zander's room. Avoiding him for three days had made the situation incredibly awkward. She crept through her room, lights off, intent on silence. Stumbling over a pair of shoes, she dropped her purse with a thud and fell on the bed. *Damn it.*

Silence reigned. Followed by a knock on the interior door. Her fingers tangled in her necklace. She was the one who'd caused the awkwardness. She couldn't avoid him forever. Throat dry, she flipped the lock and pulled the door open.

He wasn't wearing a shirt. Sculpted muscles defined his arms, chest, and stomach. She wouldn't allow her gaze to dip lower, and focused on his face and the scowl darkening his features. He rested his hand on the frame. "Where were you?"

Of all the things she'd expected him to say, that hadn't been one. "Excuse me?"

"You've been gone for hours. No one knew

where you were."

"I told Irisa this morning that I was going off the grid today."

His eyes narrowed and his gaze traveled over her from head to toe and back again. "It's not safe for you to be off the grid and out this late alone… Unless you weren't alone."

"Of course I was. I don't know anyone in this city."

"The Riptide and your buddy Slade are in town to play the Fleet."

"What does that have to do with anything? I haven't spoken to Slade since we all went to dinner."

"Torres was here earlier to pick up Irisa. When I couldn't find you, I assumed you were out with Slade."

"Well, I wasn't. I took off today because needed a break from everything in the tour."

The dark look on his face deepened. "You've been distant with me since we arrived at the hotel. I wondered if you were pulling away from me because you were starting something with him."

"That's ridiculous."

He shifted his stance. Broad shoulders filled out the doorway, showcasing his strength. "Is it? Then tell me why every time I try to get you alone, you shrink away or come up with an excuse?"

"Because that kiss was a mistake. We shouldn't have done it. We work together. I've seen this a thousand times and it never works out. I don't want to be a groupie fling." She dragged a hand through her hair. The intensity of her body's responses to him scared her. The risks of falling for him were too big to be outweighed. "And even if I did, you overwhelm me. I have a job to do, and between you and some other people, I already have enough distractions to make my job difficult."

His brows rose and one hand came up to rub the back of his neck. His lips formed a line. The flare of anger faded, but she glimpsed the bewildered hurt seconds before a mask devoid of feelings slipped in place. "I didn't realize I was causing you so many problems. I won't bother you anymore unless it's about the shows."

He stepped back into his room, then eased his door closed. The doorknob dug into her palm. Jayne released her grip. Anger and frustration coursed through her. She'd hurt him, and that hadn't been her intention.

Something slammed in his room. She strained to listen. Rustling, and then the sound of another door closing. She hurried to the door leading to the hall and looked through the peephole. Zander strode past, dressed in workout gear.

What the hell was he doing? Was this because of her? She had to fix it. She scrambled to tug on her shoes, then grabbed her keycard and phone and left the room. At the end of the hall, the elevator doors closed. He hadn't seen her, but she needed to find him.

She needed to apologize.

***

He hadn't meant to push her. Furious with

himself, Zander strode through the lobby. She'd looked too damn good, standing framed in the doorway, with the bed behind her, begging to be rumpled. All day long, he'd waited to talk to her. For days, he'd ached to touch her. He'd thought they were on the same page after that kiss.

Apparently not.

Her actions of the past few days had confused him—mixed signals and awkward conversations. Tonight, her words had cut more than he wanted to let on. He'd never forced a woman, and had never, to the best of his knowledge, made one want to hide.

Going for a run at night in an unfamiliar city wasn't the smartest thing he could do, but no way could he stay in that room, not with her only a few feet away, and not with the disappointment and frustration swirling in his blood.

The night clerk smiled at him from behind the desk. "Sir, can I help you?"

He shook his head. "Can't sleep. Going for a run."

"Our exercise room is equipped with everything you might need."

Not everything... Still, it would be safer. "Thanks."

The elevator pinged and he turned at the sound of heels clicking over the floor.

Jayne paused a few feet away. She gripped her necklace in her hand. "Where are you going?"

"I could ask you the same thing." He moved toward her, away from the clerk's prying ears. "Go back upstairs. Get some sleep."

"I can't sleep. I've hurt you and I didn't mean to and I'm sorry. This whole thing turned out wrong."

What had—their upstairs conversation? The avoidance? He needed clarification but she looked like she was about to cry. She walked past him, toward the hotel's entrance.

"Jayne."

But she didn't stop. The doors glided open and she disappeared through them. Muttering a curse, he moved toward the door.

"Sir, is everything all right?"

He ignored the clerk's question and strode onto the street. Jayne's hair swayed in the breeze. He took off after her. "Hold up."

Spotlighted under a street lamp, she turned, still worrying the delicate gold chain with her fingers.

"Where are you going?" He shoved his hands into his pockets.

"I don't know. I need to walk."

"Fine." He fell in step beside her.

She stopped. "What are you doing?"

"This isn't pushing myself on you. It's late. You're crazy if you think I'm letting you walk by yourself at night."

"I thought you were upset with me."

"Doesn't mean I'm going to let you run around out here alone."

"So you *are* upset, then." She pressed her lips together for a moment. "I think you misunderstood what I said upstairs."

He shrugged as though it didn't matter. "You want me to leave you alone, I'll leave you alone."

She made a strangled noise and turned away,

then faced him again. "Zander. I don't want to fight or give you mixed signals, but I'm really struggling with this thing between us."

A small shard of hope shed light onto his heart. "Talk to me."

"I never get involved with a client. But then we kissed and I keep thinking about that kiss and how much I want to do it again. But I wasn't hired to kiss you."

"I'll have to talk to my sister about adding that into the job description."

She granted him a brief smile. "It's more than that. I admire what you're doing for Dalton, and how you are with your dog, and your sister, and your fans."

"So what's the problem?"

"I don't do casual hook-ups."

He suppressed a grin. Good news to know. "Look, I don't do casual hook-ups either. I know rock stars have a reputation, but I've been at this job for over ten years. What's fun when you're twenty is stale when you're thirty."

Her head tilted and she studied him for a long moment. "So, then you're saying…what? You want a relationship?"

As long as he was touring, he didn't think he had a chance at a strong, long-term relationship. He'd spend years wanting what his parents had, a long-lasting marriage, but felt like that wasn't in the cards for him because of his chosen career. "I want to explore this thing between us."

"Mixing business with pleasure is a bad idea." But she didn't sound nearly as certain about that as she had before. Her body leaned into his space. She didn't touch him, but damn it, he could smell her perfume and see her darkened gaze.

That kiss—that chemistry—he couldn't deny the way Jayne made him feel. "I agree with you. So business and relationships can't work, but I can't help that I'm so attracted to you. We'll see each other nearly every day for the next two months. That's a damn long time to be fighting our attraction. Fighting it will turn it into a bigger distraction. Giving into it would be a good release. Would you be willing to be in an exclusive relationship for the duration of the tour?"

She bit her lip. "When it's over, we go our separate ways. No one gets hurt."

"Absolutely. I never want to hurt you. I think we could both make each other feel really good."

With a shaky breath, she nodded. "No one would know, right? Not even Irisa."

He banked his annoyance. Hiding things wasn't his style, but her comfort meant more than anything. "Of course not. I don't want to ruin your friendship with her."

Her hand closed over her pendant again. She let it slip through her fingers. "Okay, then. I agree."

Thank God she'd agreed to give them a chance. "You said you kept thinking about kissing me again. Are you still thinking about it?"

"Maybe." A shy smile graced her lips.

"Good." Desire thudded a low beat in his blood. He cupped her shoulders and backed her against a palm tree, away from the direct light of the lamp post. Her hands rested on his waist. He trailed his fingertips over her collarbone and up the sides of her neck, and cupped her face in his hands. She strained toward him. Achingly slow, he lowered his head, degree by degree, taking in how her eyes darkened and fluttered closed, how her breathing slowed, and how her lips parted in anticipation.

When his lips closed over hers, the feel of her was even better than he'd remembered. So soft and so sweet. He brushed his thumbs over her cheeks and dived in for another taste. Jayne's hands glided up his torso and slipped to his back. She pressed him closer. Soft curves molded to his body. Groaning, he clamped a hand to her hip and slid his other hand to the back of her head. His fingers itched to shove away the barriers separating them and discover every inch of her, but he enjoyed the sweet torture they created.

A car drove past, its headlights illuminating them for a moment before their surroundings fell back to semi-darkness.

Jayne eased her mouth away from his. "We shouldn't be doing this on the sidewalk."

"We can move it to one of our rooms."

Her hand came up to rest on his chest. "I'm not ready to rush into sex."

Locked together, he couldn't hide his body's reaction to her, and from her words, she'd noticed. "Who said anything about sex? I was talking about playing Scrabble."

"Zander." His name came out part laugh, part groan.

Laughing, he nipped her lip. "I want to get to know you. There's no pressure for anything else."

He released his hold. Leaving her curves and her heat was hard. Not ready to lose contact, he reached for her hand. It curled into his, hesitant, and then more secure in its grip.

"Let's walk on the beach. We should have it to ourselves." He guided her around the large building. The back of the hotel faced the beach. Floodlights kept the area bright. They could walk in safety and he could hold her close while warm winds danced, waves crashed, and stars winked across the darkened sky.

"Zander, Jayne. Wait up." Brendan jogged out of the hotel with Landry close behind. Damn it, so much for being alone with her.

Jayne stiffened and let go of his hand. "Is Luke with you?"

Landry tossed a football toward Zander. "He's in his room, being a grumpy ass. Want to play?"

He made the easy catch, then lobbed it back. "Nah. We'll sit here and watch."

Jayne smiled at him and lowered herself to the sand. He claimed the spot next to her, fingers resting against hers, hidden from view by the cover of sand. The feel of her fingers against his was as erotic as her lips and tongue had been. He traced patterns across the back of her fingers, rubbing soft skin amid rough grains.

She sighed and flexed her hand under his, then turned hers so palm met palm and her fingers could tease him too.

Brendan and Landry splashed through ankle-deep water. Diving catches, balls deliberately overthrown, they reminded him of the old days, when everything was simpler with the band.

Movement at the corner of his vision caught his attention. His sister walked toward them. She looked happy but Dom wasn't with her.

Jayne tried to untangle her hand from his, but he held tight and burrowed them further in the sand. "How's Dom?"

A smile bloomed on his sister's face. "Fine. Where's Luke?"

"In his room. He didn't want to come."

She chatted with them for a few more minutes about her date and then left, saying she'd check on Luke.

Soon, she rejoined them with Luke in tow. "I want some shots for your fan page. Come on, play two-on-two and make sure to stay close enough for the floodlights to catch you. And Jayne, you can take some pictures too, so we're not posting the exact same ones."

Stifling a sigh, Zander rose and brushed the sand from his hands. Usually he paired with Luke when they played. "Same teams?"

Luke shrugged. "Sure."

Irisa held up her phone. "Remember, you're supposed to be having *fun* in these pictures. It wouldn't kill you all to smile."

Zander covered Brendan while Luke tried to block Landry's throw. The spiral arced toward the drummer. He spun, then leapt for the ball and Zander ended up wrestling him for it as waves crashed around them. They reset. He had the ball. Rather than throwing, he ducked around Brendan. Landry barreled down on him. Bracing for the hit, he threw a lateral pass to Luke but the bassist caught him with a shoulder to his ribs anyway. They ended up on the ground. Zander flung wet sand at him in retaliation.

Landry smiled. "Always follow through with the tackle."

"Not when I don't have the ball anymore." He stood, and waved Luke over. "We need to take him down."

Luke didn't smile like he normally would have, but he nodded. "One more play, then I'm heading in."

Brendan threw the ball. Instead of trying to block, Zander went after Landry and Luke attacked from the opposite side. The three of them fell into the waves.

"These are great." Irisa's voice carried over the breeze. "I think I have enough."

"I think I've had enough too." Landry splashed water at him. "Wait for payback."

"Game over." He grinned. Cold seeped into his skin. Wet clothes clung to his body. Zander caught Jayne's smile and something in him warmed.

When the group reached their floor, the logistics of staying so close to the band, and wanting to be with Jayne, and her insistence to keep things a secret, hit him. Thank God they had adjoining rooms.

He went into his room, and rapped his knuckles against the interior door. Her door opened immediately, as though she'd been expecting him.

A fine coating of sand and his soaked clothes kept him from wrapping her in his arms. He traced his finger from her temple to her chin, and then tilted her chin up as he bent his head, his mouth seeking her lips.

Jayne's soft hands grasped his forearm, holding her to him. Their kiss continued, deepened to hot, and then eased back to sweet.

His heart beat quickened. The song lyrics he'd been struggling to compose suddenly filled his head. Every single word.

She laid her hand against his cheek. "It's late, and I'm sure that sand isn't comfortable. I'll let you go so you can shower."

"Good night." After one more taste, he eased back and they closed the doors between them.

Energy sparked with the need to write. The guys weren't stupid, once they heard the lyrics, they might put two and two together and figure out Jayne was his muse. But he couldn't *not* share the song.

He'd just have to take his chances.

CHAPTER EIGHT

The pub pulsed with music and laughter. The after-concert crowd had thickened once word spread that The Fury had arrived. Jayne stood by the bar, sipping her drink and chatting with Irisa. After a week on the road, she was happy to be home and back in her own bed for a few days. Her friend had invited Dom to the band's first L.A. show. The ballplayer and Zander traded stories while signing autographs and posing for pictures. Fans wandered between them and to the opposite side of the room where Brendan, Landry, and Luke hung out by the pool tables.

She swallowed her whiskey and her frustration. No matter what she did, Luke still treated her with a coolness impossible to mistake for friendliness. After five shows and countless hours with the band, she'd hoped something would have changed.

Beside her, Irisa hissed a breath. "It's good to be home, but I'd thought tonight would have gone differently."

"Dom's pretty popular." There seemed to be as many baseball fans as Fury fans.

"I'm glad he came and is getting time to talk to Zander, but it's like the flow of fans never stops. I'd like to spend time with him too."

"I'm sure things will calm down soon." Jayne patted her shoulder. As she spoke, Dom turned toward them and took a step in their direction. "See?"

To give her friend some privacy, she moved to the other end of the bar and signaled for another drink. People-watching for a while relaxed her.

Warm hands settled on her waist. She stiffened, ready to throw an elbow into whoever held her. Then Zander's scent surrounded her and she relaxed into his hands and twisted toward him. "I'm glad it's you. I was about to break into self-defense mode."

"I wondered where you went." He smiled and leaned in and brushed a kiss over her lips.

"I thought I'd give your sister and Dom some space. And I didn't want to crowd you while you were with your fans." The band's strict "no groupies" policy backstage during the tour meant every bar, restaurant, airport, and venue parking lot turned into fan events.

"I think I've spoken to every person in this place. Except you." He slid his hands across her stomach and drew her body against his solid wall of muscles.

She sipped her drink, enjoying the burn of the cinnamon flavor. His hand covered hers and he raised the glass to his lips. Less than a week had passed since their conversation by the beach. Keeping their blossoming relationship under wraps was harder than she'd expected. She liked touching him and kissing him too much.

He passed the glass back to her and she finished it off. The burn of the alcohol was nothing compared to the fiery desire in Zander's gaze.

"Dance with me."

"But someone could see us and—"

He pressed the warm pad of his finger against her lips. "The dance floor's crowded and believe me, my guys won't be out there. But they could come up here any time for a drink. We'll keep it friendly but I want to hold you. It's been a damn long day."

She couldn't argue with that.

He stopped in a shadowed space and drew her into his arms. Not as tight as some of the couples around them, but close enough for her to breathe him in and enjoy the warmth of his arms.

A thunderous crash drowned out the music. Angry male voices rang out from the direction of the pool tables.

Zander's hand tightened on her shoulder. "Goddamn it. Luke's involved."

The singer stood toe to toe with a giant biker. And then the biker's fist flew and the crowd swallowed them from view.

"Shit. Find my sister and get outside." He nudged her in the direction of the exit and then ran toward the fight.

Glass shattered and more people yelled. She dodged people and tables, searching for Irisa. No luck.

Chaos broke out around her as the fight spilled out into the rest of the pub. The biker's friends and Luke's supporters, including Zander, Brendan and Landry, jumped in.

She couldn't leave—not with them involved

and not without Irisa.

To her left, Zander threw punches with two different men. Her stomach lurched. If she couldn't find Irisa, she'd try to help him. She rushed by the bar. Someone huge barreled into her side, knocking her off her feet. She flung out her arms and grasped at air. Sickening fear shot through her. Her head smacked into the bar top. Pain exploded and the floor rushed up to meet her.

The fall knocked her breath out of her. Gasping, she clung to a bar stool. Around her, things calmed down as bouncers tossed out patrons.

Zander knelt beside her. He had a gash on his cheek and blood on his shirt. With gentle fingers, he turned her head toward him. "Are you okay? Damn it, you're bleeding and you already have an egg forming on your forehead. Can you stand?"

"I think so." She held onto his arms and allowed him to lift her. The room spun.

He dumped ice from a glass onto a bar towel and held the bundle to her head.

A black-clad bouncer came up to them. "You were in the fight. You're getting tossed. Let's go."

Her head throbbed. She leaned into Zander. He kept his arm around her and they followed Landry and Brendan. Irisa and Dom followed. The bouncer shut the door behind them.

When the band met at the middle of the parking lot, a few of the bikers came forward, looking ready to finish the fight. Zander drew her to the side farthest away. "I swear, if they take one step this way…"

"God, I hope not."

"Don't worry, I'll protect you."

Thankfully, it didn't come to that. After tense moments, Dom stepped in between the groups and managed to talk the guys down.

Relief eased some tension from her muscles but her head still hurt. She wasn't dizzy or nauseous, but laying down seemed like a very good idea.

Dom had his arm around Irisa. Her friend clutched her wrist. "We're going to the hospital. You need an x-ray."

"We'll meet you there." Zander rubbed Jayne's shoulder. "She hit her head pretty hard on the bar."

During the drive, he kept touching her hand or her knee and asking if she was okay. After the fifth time she'd reassured him she was fine, he sighed a long expulsion of breath. "I'm sorry."

"It wasn't your fault. You didn't bang into me."

"You should've gone outside when the fight broke out."

"I couldn't find Irisa, and then you guys all were fighting. I couldn't walk away."

He nodded, eyes weary and mouth turned down. "I guess I can't argue with that. I couldn't walk out on Luke."

She'd seen their bond. The way he and Luke could communicate almost intuitively. Even with the tension between them, their friendship obviously ran deep.

Zander stayed with her in the ER while the doctor ran tests, keeping her company and keeping her calm until the nurse took him away to bandage the cuts on his face and hand.

Finally, the doctor released her. She found

Irisa, Dom, and Zander in the waiting room. "I'm cleared to go home."

"What did they say?" Zander craned his neck to read the sheet. "Concussion aftercare?"

"Just as a precaution. I don't exhibit signs of a concussion so they don't need to keep me overnight. The doctor told me to take it easy for the next twenty-four hours. It's good we don't have a show tomorrow night."

His fingers gripped the paper. "This also says someone's supposed to wake you regularly throughout the night."

She met his gaze. Would he volunteer? He opened his mouth but before he could speak, Irisa stood. "Jayne can stay with me tonight."

"Are you sure you don't mind?" Her friend's bandaged wrist probably hurt like hell. Maybe she'd be able to help her, too. If nothing else, they could feel miserable together.

"It's the least I can do."

When they reached the parking lot, Zander pulled her behind a large mini-van while Dom fussed over making Irisa comfortable. "Call me if you need anything."

She grasped his hand. "Will you be okay?"

"Please, you think these little scratches will slow me down?"

For the first time in hours, she smiled. "Of course not, Mr. Indestructible."

He cupped her cheek and pressed a kiss to her forehead. "Not entirely indestructible. I do have one weakness." He stroked the bandage covering her temple with his thumb.

"What's that?"

Zander caressed the underside of her chin with a rough finger. "You."

The throbbing of her head was forgotten and so was the need to keep their relationship quiet. She wrapped her arms around his waist and pressed herself into his solid warmth. Watching him throw and receive punches in the fight, she'd realized she cared about him. More than was wise, and sooner than she'd ever fallen for anyone else. And that scared her.

He took her hands from his waist, keeping them in his, as he took a step back. "I'll see you tomorrow."

"Tomorrow." She had an entire night to think about whether ending their relationship early would be for the best.

***

By the next morning, the fight was all over the internet and the label wasn't happy. Zander didn't give a shit about those things as much as the three guys nursing injuries in his practice room. They were supposed to be practicing, but instead of drumsticks, microphones, or guitars, they held ice packs, heating pads, and bottles of pain relievers.

"Hell of a fight last night." Zander tossed fresh ice packs to Luke and Landry. They sat at opposite ends of the couch, with a snoring Shredder between them on the middle cushion.

"Crazy bikers." Luke shook his head. The purple bruise around his eye looked painful.

"Thanks for having my back."

"We couldn't leave it eight-on-one." Landry smirked. His torn-up, swollen knuckles looked like he'd put his fist through glass. "You're good, but you're not that good."

Brendan stretched out on an overstuffed chair with a heating pad over his left side. "What happened with Jayne and Irisa at the hospital? Are they okay?"

Zander rubbed his hand over his face. Every time he thought about Jayne's head hitting the bar, he wanted to punch someone. "Irisa has a sprained wrist and Jayne was evaluated for a concussion, but they let her go home."

He'd texted her that morning and she'd responded that she was okay. 'Okay' didn't tell him a whole lot.

Footsteps echoed down the hall. He was expecting his housekeeper, but Irisa came through the door. "How's everyone feeling today?"

"Fine." Zander shrugged. He wouldn't complain about his cuts, the sore wrist, or the large bruise on his thigh. He'd toughened out worse fights in the school yard.

Brendan touched his ribs. "Got some bruises from last night, but nothing that'll keep me from drumming."

Landry flexed his fingers. "I'm still icing, but should be fine by tomorrow night."

Luke removed the ice pack he'd held to his eye. "Now that we've all determined everyone's fine, what's the word from Excite? Did you have to assure them that their investment was fine?"

"Oliver did ask about your condition, and yes, they'd like you guys to refrain from making poor decisions."

Zander cracked a smile. "Really? That's what Oliver said?"

Replacing the pack, Luke laid his head on the back of the couch. "I can't believe Excite keeps that whiny ass-kisser around."

Irisa surveyed them with a sympathetic smile. "Take the day off, no practice, just rest. Keep icing things. I'll see you tomorrow."

"You're heading out? I'll walk you." Zander followed her from the room. When they reached his kitchen, he stopped her. "How's Jayne?"

"She's okay. Nothing odd. She's back at her place now. I told her to rest all day, and to skip tomorrow's show if she needs to."

"I couldn't get to her in time." He finally said it out loud.

"What are you talking about?"

"Last night, at the bar. The fight started and some guy slammed into her. I saw her going headfirst into the bar and it was like everything was suddenly in slow motion. If I'd been five seconds faster, it wouldn't have happened."

She pressed her lips together and studied him for a moment. "Is something going on between you two?"

Hell, he wasn't going to lie. "Something." He shrugged and tugged his hand through his hair. "I don't know what to call it. She's different from the other women I've dated."

"Just be careful."

Shit. Jayne didn't want anyone to know yet. "Don't say anything to her, okay? It's too new. No one knows. I don't want to upset her. Or scare her off."

"I promise." She patted his shoulder, then glanced at her phone. She typed something and then smiled. "I have to go. Maybe you should call Jayne."

As soon as the band left, he loaded Shredder into the car. Forget a phone call—they were making a house call.

One of her neighbors held open the security door for him. When he reached her apartment door, he crouched beside Shredder. "No loud barks, okay? She might need quiet."

A grumble responded. Satisfied, he knocked.

Jayne opened the door. She wore a bright pink t-shirt and soft gray yoga pants. Her hair flowed around her shoulders. Her smile brightened his mood. "Hi."

"We thought you might need some company." He waited while she slowly bent to greet the dog. Then, he handed her the bouquet of yellow and pink flowers he'd bought on the way.

"They're beautiful. Thank you." She sniffed the blooms. "I'll grab a vase from the kitchen."

He followed her through the living room. A white couch in the center was balanced by a piano on one side of the room and a desk on the other. Shredder padded beside him.

Jayne came back and placed the flowers on her desk. She moved a little slower than normal. "You can let him off his leash."

He did, and Shredder ambled to a patch of sunlight under a picture window. Zander crossed to her. His hands framed her face and he brushed the white bandage on her temple. Then he lowered his head and gently touched his lips to hers. "How are you feeling?"

"I'm a little sore and my heads hurts a bit, but no other issues. I'm fine, really."

"I'm not."

Immediately, her hands lifted to his chest. "Where are you hurt?"

He shook his head. "You scared me. I keep replaying your head hitting the bar. I'm sorry I couldn't get to you in time."

"Like I told you last night, it's not your fault. Besides, you were busy helping Luke. How are the guys?"

"Banged up, but nothing serious."

"And you. Are you really okay?" Her hand skimmed the scratch on his cheek.

"You could kiss it better."

She smiled and rose on her toes. Her lips touched his cheek. Then she kissed the cut on his hand. "Anywhere else?"

"I can think of a few other places that are aching."

Instead of the flirty retort he'd been expecting, her smile faded and she moved her hands to her sides. "We need to talk."

"What's wrong?"

"I was scared watching you squaring off against those bikers." She paced to the couch and turned. "Maybe this is moving a little to fast."

"What is?"

"Us."

"Too fast? I've been on a slow burn for weeks." He followed her over. "Is this about the fighting? The band really doesn't get into scrapes. I'm not a guy who goes out looking for fights."

"It's not that. I'm glad you stood up for your friend." Her fingers twisted her necklace pendant back and forth in her hand. "It made me see that I, well, I care about you."

"Oh." Something between satisfaction, anticipation, and relief swelled within him.

"And that wasn't part of the deal, so—"

"Hold up there." He captured her hand in his. "We never said 'no caring about the other person.' All we said was that we'd be involved during the tour. I cared about you before I suggested our arrangement."

"You did?" Wide blue eyes met his gaze. "You do?"

"I wouldn't get involved with someone I didn't care about."

"Oh." Echoing his earlier statement, she regarded him with a serious gaze. A faint blush colored her cheeks and a slight frown marred her forehead. "But we promised each other at the start that no one would get hurt. Caring means getting hurt."

That line right there told him all he needed to know. "Caring also means doing your damn best to make sure the other person doesn't get hurt."

Eyes wide, head tilted back to hold his gaze, she looked so vulnerable. "Zander."

She was thinking too much and he was tired of thinking. He needed to hold her. "Trust me. I won't hurt you."

After a long moment, Jayne laid her hand on his chest, over his heart. "All right."

Relief eased his muscles and he drew her into his arms. "Now, back to those aches…"

"Yeah?" With a blood-stirring smile, she slid her hand to his stomach, and then to his waistband. "Am I getting warmer?"

He sucked in a breath and held back a groan and then closed his hand over hers. Tempted to drag it lower, he moved it to his chest. "Today's about you. And I can tell you're sore, so we're taking it easy. What can I do? Rub your shoulders? Make you tea? I'm not much good at kitchen things."

"The shoulder rub would be nice. I hit my back in the fall too." She pointed to a low spot by her hip.

He wrapped his arms around her and pressed his fingers into the spot. Rubbing in small circles, he tried not to get distracted by the indent of her waist and how it flowed into the curve of her hip. He averted his gaze the sofa table behind her where she'd placed several framed photos of a Yorkshire Terrier. "Is that Pepper?"

"Yep. I know, I took a lot of photos, but she was so cute."

He leaned closer to examine them. In nearly every one, the dog wore a colorful top. "She let you dress her up?"

"She loved sweaters. I'm guessing from your tone that you either don't or can't do that with Shredder."

"I'm lucky he doesn't try to remove his collar." He moved his hands to her shoulders. No photos of people who could be her parents, but there were two of Irisa and Jayne, and a few of Jayne with volunteers from the animal shelter and the community center.

She laid her head on his shoulder. "This feels so good. Thank you."

His fingers skimmed up her back to massage her neck. "Tomorrow kicks off two weeks on the road so if you're not feeling up to it tomorrow night, you can rest at the hotel instead of coming to the show. Longer trips can be tough."

"I'll be fine. I don't want to leave more work for Irisa. She has enough to deal with." The way she spoke hinted that she knew more about his sister than she'd always let on.

"Last night in the ER while you were still getting checked out, she admitted she's been popping antacids a lot to deal with stress."

"She's been taking them for months. I've asked her about them before."

He lowered his hands before his frustration could tighten his hold. "You knew. Torres knew. I see her all the time and had no idea."

"You can't know everything. Considering how protective she is of you and the band, she probably hid it so you didn't worry." Jayne brushed her hand through his hair. Gentle and soothing, and exactly what he needed.

He slid his arms around her waist. "I'm supposed to be making you feel better, not the other way around."

"You are making me feel better. You brought me flowers and a dog." She traced her fingers over the faded logo on his chest. "Can you stay for a while?"

"For as long as you want." He could see himself staying with her for years, but he'd make the most of the time they had together because when the tour was over, it would have to end.

CHAPTER NINE

Five days into the road trip, Jayne finally felt like her old self. The cut on her head had mostly healed and the swelling was gone. Zander had been right about things being tough, but her problem had been the tension that ebbed and flowed between the guys—and Luke and his increasing list of "forgotten items".

The radio station hummed with excitement. She watched the contest winners file in for the band's on-air five song set. She checked the food table and confirmed all of the band's requests were laid out in front of her.

"I have a surprise for you." Zander's voice caressed the back of her neck and she shivered.

He'd been extra-excited all day. She'd known something was up. "What is it?"

"We're performing my new song. It'll be the first time anyone outside the band has heard it."

"I can't wait." Although she knew the melody by heart, he'd kept the lyrics a secret.

In his reaching for a water bottle, he trailed his fingers over her hand. "You know, you were the inspiration for it."

"I was?" She smiled shyly and fought the heat of a blush. Her? Inspiration? For that beautiful piece? Warmth spread through her chest and she placed her hand on his arm—not caring if anyone could see them. "Now I really can't wait to hear it."

"You'll be waiting a little longer. It's the last song in the set."

She smiled. "I know it'll be worth it."

He waved to a few of the fans. "We're supposed to start soon. I'll see you later."

She was still smiling after he walked away.

Luke approached in his usual attire, wearing dark jeans, a dark shirt, and a scowl. "I left my scarf at the hotel. You'll have to pick it up."

No, no, no. She couldn't risk missing Zander's song. "The temperature feels fine in here. You won't need it."

His gaze hardened. "A fan made it for me. She's here and I told her I'd wear it."

"Can't you just tell her you forgot it?"

"No. She went to a lot of trouble. We never disappoint our fans." He pointed out a pretty woman, fairly young, wearing an animal rescue center's sweatshirt. "You're the tour manager. It's your job to do things like this."

Her gaze flicked to Irisa. Her friend had been barking out orders and finding fault with everything since they'd arrived on Saturday. Out of character for her patient friend, obviously something had happened between her and Dom. But she refused to talk about it and cringed at the mention of his name. If Jayne refused, Luke might ask Irisa, and she couldn't bear to see him push her friend into snapping.

"Fine. I'll go." If she hurried, she might make it

back in time to hear Zander perform.

He handed over his keycard. "It's a black and green crocheted scarf. I think it's on the desk."

"All right."

She called for a cab, but the late afternoon rush hour had begun. Walking the eight blocks to the hotel would take twenty minutes and was faster than waiting for the cab to arrive. She half-walked, half-jogged to the hotel, and arrived puffing air and sweating, then jogged to his room. No scarf on the desk. No scarf on the bed or the floor. She peeked in the closet and the open suitcase. No luck.

Huffing out a sigh, she sent him a text. *It's not anywhere that I can see.*

His reply came a minute later. *Never mind. Found it here. Going on air now.*

Anger bubbled over. She was going to kill him.

After a quick stop in her room to change her sweat-soaked shirt for a dry one, she sprinted down the hall and two flights of stairs to the lobby. A cab pulled up to the curb. Maybe her luck was turning. She hopped in and rattled off the station's address.

Frustration built as the minutes ticked by and traffic crawled along. She abandoned the cab with four blocks to go and jogged the rest of the way.

She dashed inside the station's lobby, but several people wearing Fury t-shirts were leaving.

No. She couldn't be too late.

The band and some crew members rounded the corner, gear in hand. Sure enough, Luke had the scarf slung around his neck like a gym towel.

"Where did you find it?"

"In my microphone kit."

How did he miss checking there?

Zander met her gaze and his frown deepened and then lessened. "I'm sorry you missed the show."

"Not as sorry as I am." Did he look at someone else when he sang her song? Had he been thinking of her at all?

The car they'd hired to transport them arrived. She climbed in beside Irisa and shook her head against the sting of tears building behind her eyes. Blinking fast, nails biting into her palms, she managed to keep her emotions in check.

Brendan leaned over the seat. "Who wants to grab dinner? There's an Italian restaurant a few blocks from the hotel."

A chorus of agreements echoed from the band.

Irisa shook her head. "No thanks. I have some calls to make."

"Not me, either." Jayne glanced down at her shirt. It clung to skin that felt sticky and sweaty. She needed a shower and a big glass of red wine. Maybe two. Room service was in her future.

Zander inclined his head. "Maybe I'll stay in, too. We can grab food at the hotel's bar."

"No, please, go ahead with the guys. I think I'll take a nap. I had quite a bit of exercise today." He'd wrangled the room adjoining hers. If he stayed, she wouldn't be able to break down. She needed a few minutes to herself.

The car dropped Irisa and her off first. After bidding good night to her friend, she rushed to her room. Tears burned prisms into her vision. She swiped her cheeks and transferred some of the mascara onto her fingers. She left her clothes in a heap on the bathroom floor and turned on the shower. Steam rose, a white mist in the room. The last time he'd played the song, she'd recorded it. She left the bathroom door ajar and set up her phone right outside, with the volume on the highest setting. With Zander's song on continual repeat, she stepped inside the stall, soothed by the pounding water and a good cry.

***

Zander strode down the hall to his room. Jayne's comment about the nap and the exercise had confused him. Exercise? She'd looked upset when she'd returned to the radio station, and that look remained until they dropped her off at the hotel. When the car dropped off the guys at the restaurant, he'd begged off and requested a return to the hotel. He should have insisted on staying with her. He needed to see her.

Music came from her room. He eased his interior door open and raised his hand to knock on hers. Then paused as the melody registered.

His song.

He gave the door a light tap.

No response.

A louder tap.

No response.

Had she gone out and left the music on?

He tried her door. It wasn't locked. He slipped into the room. His music blared from her phone. The sound of the shower running drew his attention to the bathroom. Loud sobs echoed from the partially open door.

Alarmed, he pushed it open. "Jayne?"

A shriek pierced the air, loud enough to make him wince. The water turned off. "Zander? Oh my God. Don't ever sneak up on me again."

"Are you okay?" He didn't like that wobbly thread in her voice.

"What are you doing here? You're supposed to be at dinner." Her hand reached past the curtain. She groped for a towel. He handed it to her and tried not to think about the inches of exposed skin just a few feet away.

"I didn't want to be with the guys. I wanted to be with you."

The curtain moved back, revealing Jayne wrapped in a fluffy white towel.

His mouth went dry. She looked like something straight out of the fantasies he'd been thinking up since they'd met. But those red-rimmed eyes hadn't been part of any fantasy. He'd gut himself rather than make her cry. He reached for her, his hands around her shoulders. "What happened?"

"I…" She clutched the top of the towel where it tucked in at her breasts. "It's silly. I was just letting out my frustration over today. I really wanted to be there to hear your song, but Luke sent me on this errand to find his scarf—a wild goose chase for nothing. The cab was taking forever, so I jogged back to the hotel—"

"Wait. You jogged eight blocks?"

"Yeah. Then I found out that he had the scarf the whole time, then I ran back half of the way, hoping I'd get back in time to hear the song, but I arrived too late. And you never ask me for anything, but you wanted me there. I let me down and I let you down."

"Honey." He pulled her into his chest and wrapping her in his arms. He'd wanted her at the session more than anything, but his lingering disappointment disappeared when he saw how upset she was. "It's all right."

"No. It's not. I've never inspired a song before. I'm sad I didn't get to hear its debut."

"You didn't miss it. Since you weren't there, I didn't play it. We did another song instead."

"I didn't miss it?" Her head tilted back to maintain eye contact with him. Her smiled bloomed.

From the outer room, his song silenced and then began again. He lifted his finger and brushed it along her jaw line. "I guess you like my song."

"It was my favorite before I knew I inspired it."

"Why?"

"There's something about the melody."

"It gets to you."

"It makes me feel."

"I like making you feel." His other hand tangled in her hair. "I like you."

"I like you, too." A smile touched her lips. "Could you sing it to me now?"

"I think that's fair. It's your song. You should be the first one to hear it." He drew her close, wrapping his arm around her back. He swayed with her until the song began again. His heart beat hard and a little too fast. Whispering the lyrics close to her ear, he watched the way her hair moved with his breath and how goosebumps dotted her skin.

She shivered and leaned into him. Her arms came around him, holding tight. He sang the words about hearts yearning to be whole and finding the missing pieces. He moved them in a slow circle, watching their reflection in the mirror and the rightness of their bodies twined together.

He ended the song by pressing a kiss onto her neck. And held his breath as he waited for her opinion.

She arched into him, then her lips brushed his cheek. "That was beautiful. I loved it."

Her words eased the tension in his neck. He pulled back just enough to look into her eyes. Then lowered his lips to hers.

Delicate arms shifted around his torso and she returned the kiss.

Desperate to touch, his hands roamed up her sides. He cupped and teased her breasts through the terry cloth, earning a gasp from her lips, and then a moan when he skimmed a finger under the fabric.

"Zander." She wrapped her leg around his, drawing them together.

He paused with his hand over the towel's closure. "Do you want me to stop?"

She lifted her hand to his. "You better not."

With slow movements, he pulled the towel loose and it fell to the floor like a pile of snow.

"You're perfect." Both hands stroked along her skin, exploring the flares and dips. Soft skin, delicate bones, and sexy curves.

"You're wearing too many clothes." Her hands tugged at his shirt. He ripped it over his head. She grazed her nails along his arms, over his shoulders and down his torso. When her hands paused on his jeans, he looked into eyes darkened with desire. With a smile, Jayne drew his zipper down in a slow tease. His hold on her hips tightened. She nipped his lips and pushed his jeans and boxers to the floor. He sucked in a breath as she took him in her hand.

Resisting the urge to thrust, he deepened the kiss and traced patterns over her abdomen and down to her center. Jayne's head dropped against his chest while his fingers played and glided inside. She gasped and clutched him tighter. Biting his lip against the magic and friction she created with her hands, he increased the pressure and pace of his teasing until she was coming apart in his hands.

With a groan, Zander lifted his head. "Bed?"

"Now."

He paused to grab a condom from his wallet, then backed her against the mattress, following her down onto crisp white sheets.

Zander rolled on protection and maneuvered between her legs. Jayne lay spread out before him. Goddamn, he was lucky. His mouth followed the path his hands had previously taken. Lips skimming over her skin, pausing to lick and suck and nibble, he worked until she moaned and gripped his hair tight in her hands.

Breathless, she smiled. "I need you."

"Me too." Bracing himself over her, he leaned in for a kiss, then slide home. Hot, slick, tight, perfect.

Her hands squeezed into his hips. He locked her gaze to his and began to move. Faster and faster until her breath came in pants and her release constricted and eased, constricted and eased in excruciating pleasure around his shaft. Staggering pressure built and built and built, and then he gave in with a roar and followed her over.

She kissed his chest and he nuzzled in her hair while he waited for his heartbeat to level. Then he rolled onto his back and tucked her against his side. Jayne snuggled closer and linked their hands together.

He kissed her forehead. "Can I stay?"

"You better. And be ready for an encore."

***

The blare of the bedside phone's ringer jolted her awake. Jayne sat up, squinting in the darkened room.

"Ignore it." Zander's arm snagged around her waist. He pulled her down to his side.

"I shouldn't." But he was so inviting. She settled against his chest.

The ringing stopped.

"See?" His teeth nipped at her chin. Strong hands cupped her breasts and then his rough fingers tweaked her nipples.

His arousal strained against her hip. She trailed her fingers trailed down his stomach and closed her fingers around him. He groaned and thrust into her hand.

Her cell phone rang.

Zander pulled away. "Who's calling you at one o'clock in the morning?"

He picked up her phone from the bedside table. Luke's name lit across the display. "Why the hell is he calling you?"

She grabbed it and put the call on speaker. "Hey Luke, is everything okay?"

"I want a bottle of Jack. Room service doesn't have any."

What the hell? Was he serious? Did he have any idea what time it was?

Shock and annoyance flashed across Zander's features.

She plucked at the sheet. "I'll see if I can find some for you tomorrow."

"I want it now." Cold, hard, and unfriendly, he snarled the words.

Heat burned through her veins. Why did everything have to be difficult with him? Beside her, Zander shook his head, his eyes narrowed, and his hands formed fists on the bedsheets. Her own anger escalated. Tea and lozenges for performances, she could understand. Even getting the scarf so as to not disappoint a fan. But she drew the line at late-night alcohol. "Then you can call a cab if you want to go out and get it."

"We've been over this. That's not how this works. You're the tour manager. You go out and get it."

She rubbed her temples and reminded herself to be professional when all she wanted to do was reach through the phone and smack him. "Just order something else for now. If you still want it tomorrow, I'll get it for you then."

"You wouldn't want me to tell Irisa that you're

not doing your job, would you?"

Zander snatched the phone from her hand. "Listen, asshole. No one would expect her to do this. She's not going out and getting it for you. If you want it so bad, do it on your own."

Luke's voice boomed out of the speaker, "What the hell are you doing with her?"

"Never mind. Be at the breakfast bar at nine. We're having a band meeting."

"Where are you? Are you sleeping with her?"

"I'm hanging up now. And if you call Jayne again, you'll be dealing with me." He ended the call. Then turned off her phone.

She shifted, pulling the sheet higher over her breasts. "Thanks for sticking up for me."

Muscles rigid, Zander set the phone on the nightstand. "How long has this been going on?"

"What do you mean?"

"I mean, how many times has he asked you to do things?"

"It's part of my job—"

"No." His hand rested on her calf. "Late night liquor runs are not part of your job. He said you've been over this with him before. What else has he asked you to do?"

She swallowed. His question was asked in evenly spaced words, and she felt the anger behind them. "Well, you know about the scarf fiasco from today. He's also sent me on errands for throat lozenges, specialty tea, and once when he needed his portable steamer. And on Monday he wanted Guinness-flavored ice cream. I had to go to three different pubs before I found it."

"And these errands are the reasons you haven't been around back stage or at the hotel when I've come looking for you?"

"I go when he asks me to go. It's always for things he's forgotten to add to the list, or needs last-minute."

"Final question: Is he always this rude to you?"

She blinked. Zander's thunderous expression promised murder, making her hesitate. But there was no point in lying. "Always."

"Fuck. That's it." He rose off the bed and grabbed his jeans.

"Where are you going?"

"Luke and I are having a talk *now*. I'm not waiting until morning." But the look in his eyes suggested he'd be talking with his fists.

"No. Please." She jumped up and grabbed his arm. "I don't want fighting."

"No one in my band acts like this. *He's* never acted like this before. I want to know why he's being such a dick to you."

"Not everyone has to like me."

"But he damn well can treat you better. You're not his slave."

She needed to calm him down. This couldn't turn into another bar fight. She stepped in front of him, blocking the door. "It's one in the morning. You can't go pounding on his door or pounding on his head at this hour. They'll call the cops."

"I don't care."

"I do." Her mind spun. Heat glittered in his gaze. She grabbed his hand and guided it to her breast. "I'd rather have you here with me than in a jail cell."

His eyes roamed her body, his gaze became hungry and heated.

"We should pick up where we left off." She reached out and toyed with the light sprinkling of hair on his chest.

"I'm way too keyed up right now." His hands formed fists at his sides. "I can't touch you. I won't be gentle."

"Who says I want gentle?" She stepped closer then licked his chest.

"Jayne." He murmured her name. Fingers skated up her spine and cupped her shoulder. "*I* want gentle. I wanted to show you this is more than just sex for me."

Her heart melted. She turned her head and pressed a kiss into his palm. "You showed me that earlier. I know you care. You wrote me that song, remember?"

He'd sang his song to her in whispered tones as though he'd been telling her a secret, confessing his feelings, as though she was the only woman in the world he'd intended to hear it. Whether that was true or not, she needed to show him how important he'd become to her.

He drew her to him, cupped her face in his hands and touched his lips to hers. "I do care."

Her hands slipped around his waist and rested on his back. The curves of her body lined against the planes of his like they were made for each other. "Good, then stick around and show me."

Zander smiled against her lips. "All right. But I'm still ripping his head off first-thing in the morning."

The delay would only be a delay. She couldn't stop Zander from searching out Luke in the morning. But hopefully by then, tempers would have cooled.

CHAPTER TEN

Zander woke to sunlight streaming in the windows and Jayne in his arms. He stroked a hand over the curve of her waist and she laughed, shifting her body against his. He smiled and ran his fingers over that spot again. "Ticklish?"

"I know better than to answer that question." She kissed his jaw.

The alarm clock blared. He reached over and turned it off. "I have to head downstairs."

"I don't want any tension. He probably won't ask me to run crazy errands anymore." Sitting up, she grabbed his arm. Tension tightened her voice and her muscles stiffened. "I really don't want this to get worse."

He wrapped his arms around her and kissed her temple. "It's not going to get worse. I'm talking to him."

"Okay, but please don't say anything to Irisa. She has a lot going on right now. I know something happened with her and Dom and I don't want to give her anything new to worry about."

"All right. She doesn't have to know." Dom had made his sister cry. And for that, he needed to be held accountable. For now, he could leave his sister out of the situation. "Wait here for me. I don't think this will take long."

"Talking only. No fighting."

"I will do my best not to punch him but I can't make any promises."

He dressed and then headed downstairs. Landry and Brendan waited by the breakfast bar. He grabbed a cup of coffee. A few minutes later, Luke arrived.

Landry yawned. "Why are we having a meeting?"

Luke glared at Zander. "What the hell were you doing in Jayne's room? Are you sleeping with her?"

"Dude, really?" Landry shook his head. "You know it's not smart to fuck someone who's with the band."

Shit. "That's not the point of this discussion."

"Maybe it should be." Luke leaned against the wall, arms crossed over his chest.

"Hell no. Don't turn this around. Jayne's not your slave. If you forget to ask her to pick you up something when you give her the list, then you're out of luck. You wouldn't have asked my sister to run around making all these special trips for you, so you're not forcing Jayne to do them anymore either."

"What were you asking her to do?" Brendan glanced back and forth between them like he was watching a tennis match.

Luke raised his brow. "I don't see how throat lozenges are a big deal."

"One AM requests for liquor are. Demands for fucking ice cream are."

"You asked her to do that?" Brendan leaned

closer. "What's wrong with you?"

Luke scowled. "It's not that big a deal."

Zander shoved Luke's shoulder. "Like hell it isn't. You're keeping her from doing her job. And you're making her job more difficult. Also, stop being an asshole when you speak to her."

"Whatever, man. I'm done." Luke turned and strode toward the lobby.

Zander followed him. "We're not done. I don't know what your deal is, but you're going to be nice to her. And while you're at it, get your memory checked. I've never known someone to *forget* as many things as you have these past few weeks."

They gained the attention of everyone in the lobby.

Luke flipped him off and walked through the automatic doors.

Two hands on his shoulders kept Zander from following. Brendan stood on his left and Landry on his right.

"Let him go." Landry sipped his coffee. "So are you sleeping with Jayne?"

He grunted. So much for secrecy. But maybe everyone knowing was better. "Got a problem with that?"

"Not as long as it doesn't fuck up the tour. And she doesn't seem like the type for that to happen."

"Where is she? I don't like thinking she's been unhappy." Brendan scanned the room.

"Upstairs. I told her I wanted to talk to you alone. I don't know why Luke's being such an asshole."

"He's been that way since we left New York."

"Yeah well, it's going to stop now. I don't care what he says to me, but Jayne's working for us, so he'd better figure out how to put on his professional face."

When the elevator opened, he stepped inside. "I'm going to go see her."

Jayne had showered and made the bed. He kissed her and handed over his coffee. "I thought we could share."

"As long as it has some sugar in it, I'll be good."

He waited until she'd taken a sip. "Thing is, the guys know about us. Luke asked me what I was doing in your room at one AM."

"Oh."

"Brendan and Landry don't care."

"But Luke does?"

"He walked out during our meeting. But I laid into him. No more special requests. If it's not on the list, it's not happening." He paused. "Actually, I'll be taking a look at that list from now on to make sure there aren't any crazy requests thrown in."

She nodded. "All right."

He grasped her hand. "Why did you run those errands for him? Why not come to me or to my sister and tell us what was going on?"

"I've had musicians ask for odd things before, so I didn't think it was too much of a big deal at first. Then I thought that since the guys know to come to me for the requests, that maybe Irisa did the extra errands for them too. Yes, he's been an asshole to me, but I really thought things would get better. Or at least that he would become more pleasant toward me. It's crossed my mind that maybe he's doing this as a test. You know he wasn't happy when I was hired. Maybe he needs proof that I can do anything he asks."

"I don't like that thought at all. If I find out he was doing it to test you, I'll kick his ass."

"He reminds me of a stray."

"What?"

"Sometimes, when he's sitting alone, he looks lonely. When he's with you guys, sometimes he's fine and sometimes he's snappish, and when he's with me, he's in full-on non-friendly. Just like a stray dog at the shelter."

"I told him to be nicer. If he isn't, you need to tell me. You also need to tell me if he does ask you to do anything else."

"I don't want to create problems between you and your band mates."

"You're not the one who created the problem. He is."

Equipment problems sound and lighting issues plagued their shows for the next three nights. Jayne handled the glitches like a pro. To make good on his threat, Zander kept close watch on Luke and Jayne. Luke didn't talk to him unless it was necessary, and didn't even look at Jayne. Playing on stage together was difficult. Every time he looked at Luke, he wanted to throttle him. But coming back to the hotel and sinking into Jayne's softness eased his tension.

That weekend, Mother's Day presented a challenge. He'd been looking forward to flying home with Irisa to spend the day with his mom, like they did every year. But with the heightened tension, he was hesitant to leave Jayne alone in the same hotel as Luke. Brendan solved his problem, volunteering to fill in as Jayne's shadow.

When he got back to his parents' house after their annual *go-to-brunch-and-guilt-the-kids-into-wanting-kids* fun, he called Jayne.

"Hey." Her voice softened.

"What are you up to?"

"Brendan and I are hanging out." She murmured for Brendan to say hello. A *hello* called out in the background. "We went to lunch, and we're going to a movie tonight. How's your visit with your mom?"

"Great. She doesn't change." His mom had been on a you-need-to-get-married kick for years. She'd said he needed someone to take care of him. Thank God his dad was sane.

"I wish mine would." Her voice sounded wistful. "Anyway, I'll see you tomorrow morning?"

"Bright and early. Keep that bed warm for me."

"If you get back early enough, I might still be in it."

He grinned. "That better be a promise." As good as it was to be home, he couldn't wait to get back to see her.

***

The second week on the road had been tough. She'd steered clear of Luke and he'd steered clear of her but the tension between Luke and Zander was sky-high. Jayne was thrilled when the plane touched down in L.A. on Sunday morning. The rest of the tour was divided into a week at home, a week away, repeat, repeat, repeat.

Tonight, they had a charity event to attend, hosted by Dom. The band was scheduled to play, and Jayne had promised Irisa she'd be there for moral support.

She climbed into Zander's car and leaned over the gear shift to give him a kiss. "Thanks for driving me."

"Anytime."

Kate called her when they were halfway home. "Can you do me a favor? It's for Dalton."

"What's up?" Hopefully it wouldn't be a request to meet Luke. She couldn't guarantee that one. She put the call on speaker and grabbed a pen and paper from her purse.

"The apartment he and his mom are moving into doesn't allow pets, and his dad refuses to keep the dog because of how much he works. He only gets Dalton for two weekends a month."

So sad. He loved that dog. "So you want me to help Dalton take Patch to the shelter?"

"Well, I know you were thinking of getting another dog..."

Damn it. She wasn't ready yet. "Pepper hasn't been gone long. I don't think I'm ready yet."

"Please? I could hide him at my place for a little while, but I can't take him permanently. My building has a one-pet-per-apartment rule."

"What kind of dog is he?" Zander's gaze met hers for a moment before he returned his focus to the road.

"Patch is half-Boxer and half-Beagle."

"He's three years old and really cute." Kate chimed in. "Mostly white with light brown patches, and big brown eyes."

Dalton did love that dog… Her resolve weakened. She looked over at Zander. Then put herself in Dalton's place. She'd felt isolated, alone, and separated at his age. She could help Dalton, and shelters didn't need more animals.

"Please." Kate begged. "Dalton is so upset. He trusts you."

She couldn't say no. "I'd have to meet the dog first to make sure it's a good fit."

"I knew I could count on you."

After making plans to meet with Kate and Dalton, she ended the call and glanced at Zander. He watched her with a measured gaze. "You ready to take that on?"

"I can look at it like a foster situation. Maybe they'll only live in that apartment for a year, and maybe they'll move to a pet-friendly one after that."

"Or maybe you just found yourself a new permanent dog."

She shrugged. "Pepper wandered into my life at the right time. Maybe Patch is too."

He stared at the road for a while. "Mind if I tag along? I've been texting with Dalton a little bit and sending him how-to videos for playing my solo. It would be good to see him again."

Two hours later, Jayne and Zander arrived at a dog park near Zander's house. Dalton and Kate were tossing a Frisbee to Patch.

The kid wore the Fury t-shirt Zander had given

him and the saddest expression Jayne had ever seen. She crouched beside him and greeted the dog. Patch licked her hand and jumped up on her. For a moment, sadness about Pepper overwhelmed her, but then Patch barked and bathed her cheek in doggie kisses.

"Mom said she can't wait for another apartment to open up. I don't know why my dad won't keep him." Shaggy hair covered eyes she was sure were blinking back tears.

"When are you guys moving?"

"In June."

She patted his shoulder. "Well, you can come and visit him any time you want. He's still your dog. I'm just dog-sitting for a while. You can take him back any time, I promise."

"Okay." He blew out a breath and sat on the ground and pulled the dog into his lap.

Jayne backed away, giving him time alone. Tears hit the back of her eyes. She found the comfort of Zander's strong chest and leaned into him.

He looked at Kate. "I'm told the center gets all of its instruments from donations."

"That's true. That's how the music teachers come to us too. It's all volunteer so we can offer the kids the lessons for free."

"When I was starting out, I couldn't even afford new guitar strings, but when things took off and we became famous, everyone started giving us stuff for free. In the past, the band has donated instruments to schools. We have a lot of things the center might be able to use. Give me a chance to get through this tour and I'll see what I can give you."

"Jayne, I really like your friend." Kate grinned. "So, what's the verdict with Patch?"

"He's a good dog. I think it'll be fine, except for what it's doing to Dalton."

"What are you going to do when you're on tour? He's not as small as Pepper was."

"I guess I'll have to board him."

"Or he can hang out with Shredder." Zander pulled her closer. "My housekeeper takes care of him if I can't take him on a trip. And if he can't do it, my parents help out. Two dogs wouldn't be that much harder than one. Remember, Shredder's pretty lazy."

"You'd do that?" Jayne lowered her sunglasses and regarded him over the top.

"Shredder needs a buddy." With that, he strolled over to Dalton and began a discussion on music, guitars, and pets.

Kate nudged her hip. "You lucked out."

"He's pretty unreal." She smiled. He was passionate, compassionate, stubborn, and kind. But his best friend didn't like her. And she didn't pretend to think that wouldn't matter in the end.

CHAPTER ELEVEN

Zander closed the door to the dressing room. Things had been tense between Luke and him for weeks. He'd thought the tension had eased the previous evening when they'd all come together to support Irisa, but even there, Luke interpreted "be nice to Jayne" to mean "pretend she doesn't exist." Zander knew it hurt her feelings, and for that reason alone, he wanted to see her smile. "We're putting the new song in."

Luke shook his head. "I don't think so. We're all supposed to agree, and I don't agree."

"Well it's three-to-one, so you're overruled." He'd cleared it with Brendan and Landry earlier.

"I'm not having a fucking ballad mess up my fucking show."

"How would one song mess up a show?" His hands formed fists, ready to unleash his anger. "Fuck you. Go. I'll sing."

Luke laughed, then sneered. "The fans won't buy that. We can replace a bass player, a drummer, hell, even you. But you can't replace a lead singer. I'm what brings fans in."

He hadn't meant the whole damn show—but wait... "You're what brings the fans in? Just you, asshole?"

"Guys, enough." Irisa pushed between them. "You have to be onstage in a few minutes. Pull it together."

He'd had enough. Zander locked into the stare-down. Luke had become an even bigger asshole than his new normal level. "Might want to watch that ego, buddy. All of us have taken turns at the mic."

"You think you can do better than me?" Luke shoved Zander's chest. Physically, they were evenly matched. He didn't back down. "Fine. Have at it." He grabbed his jacket and slammed out of the room.

Shaking his head, Zander stared at the door. The room behind him was silent. He turned, expecting to find an ally in Brendan or Landry, but neither one looked anything but angry.

Irisa leveled them each with a glare. Shadows under her eyes sharpened her fury. "Is it too much to ask that you get along for one show?"

"I'm getting really tired of him." Rolling his shoulders, he reached for his guitar.

Landry tugged on his leather jacket. "Not only him."

Still primed for a fight, Zander faced the bassist. "What was that?"

The door opened. Not Luke. Jayne walked in, wavy hair flowing behind her. "It's show time."

"Did you see Luke?" Irisa gripped a roll of antacids in one hand and her phone in the other.

She shook her head. "Where was he going?"

Brendan moved toward the door. "I'll go look for him."

Realization dawned on Jayne's face and she put

her hand on Brendan's chest to stop him. "No. Get to the stage. I'll find him." Jayne rushed out.

"What the hell?" Zander grabbed his guitar and stalked out of the room, gaze sweeping the hallway as he made his way to the stage. If Luke delayed them...

The crowd grew restless as the minutes ticked by. He waited, anger gathering steam, and exchanged annoyed looks with Brendan and Landry.

The scent of Jayne's perfume reached him a second before she appeared by his side. "Security couldn't find him, so they checked their cameras. He walked out of the building a few minutes ago and got into a cab."

"Fuck." He bellowed the word and Jayne flinched. "He wants to leave that way? Fine."

Irisa grabbed hold of his arm. "You can't go out there and tell the fans that he walked out."

"I know, I know. He got sick." Using air quotes, he smirked.

"Make sure you don't use those hand gestures when you tell the fans," his sister urged. She had her phone out, and sent another text to Luke.

What the hell? He needed to hit something, but instead, he had to go out there and feign concern over his friend's fake illness. And Irisa would have to deal with the label. Excite wouldn't appreciate Luke walking out. The idiot could find himself in a lot of trouble.

Jayne's hand met his, cool and reassuring. He tugged her against him and pressed a kiss to her lips. She gave him a moment of calm in a storm.

His emotions evened. He held on to that feeling as he stepped on stage.

The crowd went wild. He grabbed hold of the mic. "Hey guys, how the hell are you all doing tonight?"

They responded with cheers and chants. He glanced at Landry and raised his brow. The bassist shrugged.

"So you guys probably noticed we're missing a band member. Luke's sick. He strained his voice. It was sudden and he's so sorry he can't be here with you." He bit back the snarl and waited out the mild boos. "But we're gonna give you guys a great show, and you're going to help us do it. I want you all to sing along as loud as you can. You're all honorary band members tonight."

Cheers echoed back. Maybe they could pull this off. He launched into "My Fist, Your Face," picturing Luke as he sang. For the next hour, he chatted and sang. Then he spied a young woman in the front row. She'd held up a sign that read *It's my birthday and I came here to sing with Luke.*

He had security help her onto the stage, then turned to the crowd. "She came here to sing with Luke, so how about we sing "Happy Birthday" to her?"

The crowd sang and the girl beamed. When the song finished, she hugged him, then held up her phone and they took a photo together. She squinted at her screen and her mouth dropped open. She thrust her finger in his face. "You lied. Luke's not sick. He's at a bar with my friend."

His mic picked up her words.

Boos drowned out the low tune Landry played. Fuck. Fuck. Fuck. Fuck. Fuck. Fuck.

A security guard helped the girl back into the crowd. Cursing Luke, Zander leaned into the mic. "I told you his voice was strained, guys. He couldn't perform and give you one hundred percent. That's why he's not here. But come on, let's show everyone why you're the best crowd we've had on the tour."

Fresh beads of sweat ran down his face. He turned to the guys. "Let's do "Raging Inferno"." The aggressive, fast-paced song was a fan favorite.

"Luke sucks! Luke sucks!" The crowd's chant blended into the song. And an open cup of beer landed on the stage, sloshing its contents at Zander's feet. He stepped back and dodged another, then another. Trash came flying from all directions. Security jumped onstage.

He moved closer to Landry, in front of Brendan's kit. "Keep playing."

"Refund! Refund!" The new chant grew even louder. More trash sailed his way. A container smacked into his guitar and splattered orange goo all over the pickups.

"Fuck." He whipped his head toward Chad. The tech tossed him a towel. Swiping at the substance, he stared at the sea of angry faces in the out of control crowd. Fucking nacho cheese on his fucking guitar. Seething, he motioned for the guys to stop playing and broke through the wall of security to reach his mic. "You guys want a refund? Contact Luke through Excite Records. He'll make sure you get one."

"Zander," Jayne called to him, waving her arms

for him to exit to her side of the stage. The guys from Assertive Ire stood with her. They weren't due to go on for another hour. He kicked a path to them through the debris, sending cups rolling.

Griffin jerked his head toward his band. "We're ready. We can take over from here."

Might as well turn it over to them. The crowd wasn't settling down. "Thanks, man. I'll owe you one."

The stage lights dimmed.

Show over.

He strode past his sister. "I'm going to kill him."

"Get in line." Irisa followed him away from stage and back to the dressing room. "One of you could've been seriously hurt out there."

Landry pulled off his dripping jacket and beer-stained shirt. "Where was he? Let's go get him."

"Too late." Brendan looked at his phone. "Other fans showed up there, but he's gone now."

Zander set the towel aside. He'd need something else to get the cheese out of the crevices. "As far as I'm concerned, he's out of the band."

"No rash decisions." His sister's voice was firm. "Hit the showers and let's get out of here. He's not answering any of us, so you have two choices. One, you go home, nowhere else, *home*, and we'll figure this out in the morning. Or two, you come with me to Luke's house. He has to come home sometime."

Brendan nodded at Irisa. "I'll go with you."

"Me too. I want some answers." Landry cracked his knuckles.

If he went anywhere near Luke, he'd kill him.

"Fuck him. I'm going home and making some calls. We'll replace him. Let him go."

"You can't make that decision on your own," Irisa sighed and dragged a hand through her hair. "He's not his normal self. You can't just boot him out."

The fans had wrecked the stage, he and the guys were wearing evidence of their anger, and she wanted him to feel sympathy for the bastard? "You see him here? He made his choice. I'm making the calls."

He caught Brendan's gaze. The always-joking drummer's features were set in grim lines. "Might as well. We don't know if he's coming back for tomorrow night's show either."

Jayne walked toward Irisa. "I'll come with you too, if you think it will help." She looked as bewildered and uncertain as he'd ever seen her, playing with her necklace. Volunteering to put herself in Luke's path didn't make sense, unless she was doing it as a support to his sister.

"No." Zander reached for her hand and intertwined their fingers. "Come with me. I need to feel like I have at least one person on my side."

Landry stepped in front of him. "I'm on the *band's* side. Something you and Luke seem to have forgotten lately." He moved toward the door. "See you guys there."

Brendan jangled his keys in his hand. "Landry's right. We're all out of tune."

With his sister and band mates gone, quiet descended upon the small room. Drained, frustrated, and so fucking tired, Zander gave his guitar one more inspection and then closed it in its case. He'd need to remove the strings and properly clean it when he got home. Leaning on the table, he dropped his head to his chest. Everything was so messed up.

Jayne's arms slid around his waist. Her head rested against his back. She didn't say a word. He laid his hand over hers and squeezed. Her quiet breaths and the scent of her perfume calmed him.

"I'm going to grab a quick shower."

"Want some help?"

He smiled and turned, wrapping her in his arms. "If you get in there with me, we won't be going anywhere for a long time."

"A repeat of this morning? Promise?" Blue eyes studied his face. Her hand cupped his cheek. "Are you okay?"

Flipping through a mental file of possible replacements for Luke, he pulled her closer. "I can't let what happened tonight happen again."

"Do you think you'd be able to find someone who can finish out the tour?"

"Not in time for tomorrow night's show."

"Why did he walk out tonight?"

"We had a discussion about adding in that new song."

Lines formed between her brows. "And that made him walk out?"

"I guess. That's what started it off."

"Don't you think that's a pretty strong reaction? Maybe something else really is going on with him." Her fingers moved to rest on his chest. "The first time you played the song at practice, he got angry.

When you played it in the dressing room, he got angry. When you played it at sound check, you said he walked out. Maybe something about it sets him off. Music can dredge up all kinds of memories."

"So what are you saying?"

"Despite what I've experienced, Irisa keeps telling me Luke's a nice guy. And I know you guys have been friends for years, even if things are tense right now. Maybe you should check on him before you make any phone calls."

"You think I should go to his place."

"I do."

"Even after what he did to you?"

Her shoulders lifted in a delicate shrug. "You said yourself that he's never acted this way before. It's hard, but I'm trying. You're his best friend. You can try harder. He's being a dick, but I think you're the only one he'd confide in. Even pissed off."

He pressed a kiss to her lips. She was a better person than him. "All right. Let's go."

When they pulled up outside of Luke's house, the houselights were on and Irisa's car was in his driveway. His sister must have been inside. "He's home."

Jayne nodded. She'd grown quiet during the drive.

"You can wait here if you want."

"No. I'll come with you."

Brendan and Landry parked ahead of them. The men stepped on the sidewalk.

Zander waved his hands to the friends he'd known for over a decade to wait up for him. "He's doing this stupid, reckless shit. I don't understand it."

"Me either." Brendan shook his head. "I don't even know him anymore."

Landry focused his gaze on the house. "Did you call anyone?"

"Jayne thought we should come here first. See him. Talk to him."

The bassist nodded. "Griffin told me they're having a hard time controlling Seth, but if they release him from the band they're worried he might end up in a worse place without anyone watching over him."

"Yeah, but Seth has a history of drug problems. That's not Luke's deal." Zander reached for the comfort of Jayne's hand.

Soft fingers curled around his. "None of you know what Luke's deal is yet. If you're worried about him, you can keep better tabs on him if he's with you on tour."

"True." Landry nodded again. "He's always had a temper, but not like this."

The lines of tension in Brendan's face lightened. "Then we're agreed, he stays. But now, we need to talk to him."

As a group, they approached the door. Landry leaned on the doorbell. When it opened, he pushed past Luke. "What the hell?"

Zander followed Brendan. He met Luke's gaze and fresh anger broke out again. "We want an explanation."

"I shouldn't have walked off." Luke shoved his hands in his pockets and shrugged.

"Damn straight." His heart pumped and his

nerves fired.

Landry pushed up his jacket sleeves. "We need you *on stage*, not in a fucking bar when we're in the middle of a goddamn show."

Luke glared at him. "I already said I shouldn't have walked out. I'm sorry, okay? I fucked up. Fire whoever you hired. No one's taking my place."

"You think so, huh?" Zander edged closer, searching for...*something*...regret, remorse, a hint of the old Luke.

"Yeah. I do." Luke squared off, rolling his shoulders.

"Come on, guys." Irisa pushed in between them.

"Stand down." Glaring, Brendan nudged in, forcing Luke back another step. "If one of you messes up your hands, you might not be playing tomorrow night. Cool it." He turned his gaze to Zander. "He apologized. Yeah, we're all still ticked off at each other, but let's not make this even worse."

He read the unspoken request. *Don't say something you'll regret.*

Gentle fingers brushed the back of his arm. "Come on, Zander. I don't think he's in the mood to talk. Let's go." Jayne's clear voice cut through his anger, pleading. "Let's just forget tonight happened."

"Pretty hard to forget." But he couldn't ignore the tremor in her voice. Muscles tense, he took a step back, then another, until Jayne came into his field of vision. She didn't like fighting. Sure enough, she gripped her necklace around her fingers. Her discomfort doused his need to press further. They'd keep Luke around and try to figure out what the hell was going on. He slid his arm around her shoulders. When he reached the door, he turned back to Luke. "You better show up tomorrow night."

"I'll be there." Luke crossed his arms over his chest. "Count on it."

Zander closed the door at his back. Counting on Luke didn't inspire the confidence it once had. Hopefully it wouldn't turn out to be a mistake.

CHAPTER TWELVE

Jayne was glad to see Luke arrive for sound check the next evening. Hopefully, it would prove that Zander and the guys had made the right choice. Luke had arrived with Irisa, grunted at his band mates, and ignored her. But the show went on. She stood backstage and listened to him talk to the crowd. He'd gone along with the story of his voice being strained, and told the crowd how awesome they were. The crowd was very forgiving. No thrown food or beer.

Beside her, Irisa seemed calmer. Jayne nudged her. "How are things?"

"After I left Luke's last night, I stopped at the pub in my building for a drink. I ran into Dom. We talked, and things are getting back to being okay."

"That's good. I like him." Dom seemed a lot more worthy of Irisa than Oliver had been. She wanted to see her friend happy. The less stressed, the better.

A few days later, the band flew in to San Jose. Two shows there, on Saturday and Sunday, followed by two shows in Sacramento on Monday and Tuesday.

Jayne stared at the view of San Jose from the

hotel room. Not much of a view from the third floor.

Zander dropped his suitcase on the bed. They'd done away with separate rooms. "Are you going to see your parents while you're in town?"

"I might skip it. They're probably busy."

"I'm sure they'd like to see you."

"We're not very close. But it has been a while." Feeling guilty, she made the calls and arranged to meet her dad for lunch and her mom for morning coffee. When she ended the call, she found him watching her with an odd expression on his face. "What?"

"You look stressed."

"My parents have that effect on me." She spun her pendant on the necklace chain. "Dad works for a software developer. He travels a lot for business and is on his second marriage. My mom also works with computers but on the cyber security side, and she's just divorced husband number three."

"And somehow two techies raised a musically-inclined child who makes her living traveling with rock bands." He raised his brow and smiled. She appreciated his attempt to lighten the moment.

"I didn't want to be like either one of them." She began unpacking to give herself something else to focus on.

Zander's hands clasped her shoulders. He drew her against him. "I'll come with you and be your buffer."

She laid her hands over his. "I appreciate it. I just hope you won't regret it."

On Sunday morning, they met her mother at a

coffee shop near her home. Though still beautiful, her mother's bitterness aged her far beyond her years. She vented about divorce and lawyers for a good fifteen minutes before asking Zander anything about himself or asking Jayne how the tour was going.

Finally the topic switched to the tour, but her mom wasn't ready to let go of tying everything back to her most recent ex-husband. "Hell, I couldn't trust my husband on business trips. I don't know how any musician's wife could trust her man on the road. You must know what I mean, Zander. I'm sure woman throw themselves at you all the time."

Jayne gripped her mug as heat flushed into her cheeks. "Mom."

Zander winked at her. "Well, I'd want my wife to travel with me. In fact, it would be great if she already worked in the business." Reaching under the table, he grasped Jayne's hand. "I wouldn't want long separations. The most successful relationships are the ones where spouses take an active role in each other's lives. When I get married, I want my wife with me all the time."

That quieted her mom for all of a minute. "Are you seeing your father while you're here?"

"Later today." She toyed with her coffee stirrer.

"Is he still with that tramp?"

"If you mean his wife, then yes. And I'm not talking about him."

The visit wrapped up after that.

The meeting with her dad wasn't much better. He'd arrived late, taken three phone calls, and managed to throw a veiled insult at her mother, all in under thirty minutes.

When they returned to the hotel room, she slipped off her heels and sat on the edge of the bed. "And now you see why I don't spend a lot of time with them. They're always that way. I don't understand how two people can still try to hurt each other after so many years."

Zander sat beside her. "I'm sorry I pushed you to call them."

"It's okay. They aren't like your parents. Irisa's told me how well your parents get along—how well you all get along. I would have killed for that growing up. Actually, I'd still love to have it now. I'm so tired of everything being a battle with them. They didn't divorce until I was fifteen. From the time I was little, I blamed myself for their fighting. If I'd been a better student, or a better piano player, or better daughter, then maybe they'd magically get along. But no matter what I did, it was never enough to stop the fighting."

"It's not your job to make them happy."

She nodded. "I know that now. So I put my foot down. I won't listen to them talk badly about each other. But that still doesn't stop me from getting caught in the middle."

He wrapped his arms around her. "I need to make you smile. Right now."

"You were with me today. That's enough to make me smile." She pressed her cheek into his chest, inhaled his scent, and sighed. "We have a few hours until we need to leave for the arena. Let's order room service and lounge around."

"Deal. I'll order it. Why don't you hop in the

shower? Let the hot water relax you and I'll be in soon to wash your back."

"Wash my back? Is that what we're calling it today?" She smiled and sent him a seductive glance over her shoulder before closing the bathroom door.

He joined her, but kept his touches light and teasing, and then slipped out claiming he'd heard room service arrive.

When she came out of the bath, two covered dishes were on the desk and a jeweler's box was on the bed. "What's this?"

He smiled. "Open it and see."

Nestled inside the box was a rose-gold necklace with a pink diamond heart pendant. "It's beautiful."

"I notice you touch your pendant a lot when you're nervous or anxious."

Her hand lifted to where her pendant usually hung and she laughed. "I guess I do. I never thought about it."

"Well, now when you touch this one, maybe you'll think of me, and maybe that will help you feel better. And the color reminded me of your hair."

She was touched he'd think of a gift with such meaning that showed he'd paid attention to her. "I love it. But this is too much. This is like something you'd give a wife or a serious girlfriend...not a short-term fling."

"Jayne. You're not a short-term fling."

Her heart pumped fast—a drumbeat in her chest. "But...that's what we agreed."

Zander wrapped her hand in his and drew her down to sit beside him on the bed. "I want to change that agreement. I care about you."

This seemed more serious than the *I care about you's* they'd exchanged early on. Her heart wanted to dance but her mind put on the brakes. "But…"

His grip tightened. "I want to throttle your parents. It's no wonder you're jaded. The fact that you'd even consider dating me is a miracle. Your parents' marriages haven't worked out, but that's not to say that every marriage will fail. A lot of rock stars I've known haven't had successful relationships, but that's not to say that every rock star relationship is doomed to fail. I think we should break the cycle. I want us to give it a shot. When the tour's over I'd like to keep seeing you."

The tour still had a few weeks left. And then she'd have a short vacation before Vendetta's tour would take her away from Zander for a few months. She didn't like the idea of being separated from him for such a long time. "I guess we could try."

His smile widened across his face. "That's all I'm asking. Now try on that necklace. I want to see it on you."

After fastening the necklace around her neck, she glanced at the pendant. The heart hung just above the swell of her breasts.

"You're so beautiful." Zander traced his finger around the heart, grazing her skin.

She trailed kisses over his face. He answered back with lingering kisses on her lips and fingers. Sunlight brightened the room as they fell across the bed.

She leaned into him, stroking his muscles, and tugged his shirt off. He peeled off her tank top and jeans before ridding himself of his pants and shirt.

Her underwear and bra, and his boxers quickly followed. Clothes littered the floor like confetti.

Wrapped in each other, they sank onto the bed, mouths tasting, hands teasing. She pushed him back and kissed a path from his chest to his straining arousal. He groaned as she placed a kiss on the tip, and then moaned when she took all of him inside her mouth. Her pendant swung and tapped the base of his shaft. A harsh groan sounded and Zander's hands dove into her hair. Cradling her head, he guided her movements.

"Stop." The word gasped out a moment before his hands tightened their hold.

She released him and with a smile, he tugged her on top of him. His fingers traced the line of her neck and down her back, and came to a rest at her hips before slipping between their bodies to drive her as crazy as she had driven him.

She guided him inside her and arched into warm palms and strong fingers. He sucked in a breath and closed his hands over her hips, holding her in place as she began to move. Thrusting into her, he quickened the pace. She tossed her head back as pleasure arrowed into her and she rode out the wave until it crashed, then melted onto Zander's chest.

Kissing her, he reversed their positions, and slipped her legs onto his shoulders. They watched each other as he plunged inside. She felt him deeper, felt their connection deepen, as he lost his grip on his control.

She caressed his back while his panting eased.

He smiled down at her. "When I get my energy

back, I promise I'll grab the plates."

"What did you order?"

"Pasta." He nipped at her lips and then rolled off of her. "So we can refuel and do this again."

Laughing, she kissed his shoulder, and then held up her pendant, twisting it so all the different facets caught the light.

Zander was that way—all these different sides that not everyone got to see. But she did. He'd let her in. And she loved everything she'd seen.

Loved.

The word caused a funny feeling in her chest.

He slid off the bed—confident in his own skin—uncovered the dishes then presented them, offering her first choice between Pasta alla Norma and Spaghetti Carbonara. She could imagine spending every day with him.

She loved how he made her feel.

She loved him. But instinctively knew it was too soon to tell him.

**

They had the dog park to themselves. Jayne tossed a tennis ball to Patch while Zander tried to coax Shredder with a Frisbee. They'd arrived home from Sacramento that morning to a call from Dalton's mother begging her to pick up the dog. Her landlord was letting her move in a few days early and she needed Patch gone. Dalton was still at school. Jayne didn't like the idea of just taking the dog, so Zander sent him a text, telling him to call them after school.

Shredder and Patch got along great. Patch ran circles around his less enthusiastic counterpart—jumping, playing, rolling around—and Shredder looked on like a bored teen putting up with a kid brother's antics. But Patch was happy to let the double-his-size bulldog take top dog honors.

"I think my dog has had enough for today." Zander crouched beside Shredder and rubbed his head. "I'm hoping Patch will make Shredder a little more active."

She clipped on the dogs' leashes. "We'll have to get them together for play dates."

"Or sleepovers." He leered at her and raised his brows.

Laughing, she tossed the tennis ball and Frisbee into a tote bag. "You want to have a sleepover with two dogs?"

"Well, yeah, as long as you're there too."

"I'll dig my sleeping bag out of my closet." She smiled.

He didn't laugh like she'd expected. Instead, he linked their fingers together. "Tonight?"

"I'm sure I can be talked into it if pizza, popcorn and scary movies are included."

Once they settled the dogs in the car, he wrapped his arms around her, bringing her flush against his frame. As his mouth descended, Jayne strained to meet him. Twining her fingers in his thick hair, she pressed closer and drew his lower lip into her mouth.

"Zander," a female voice called out of a car that had pulled into the lot.

Jayne released her hold. Zander had the

expression of a kid caught with his hand in the cookie jar. He looked at the woman. "Hi, Mom. What are you doing out this way?"

Jayne glanced between the two. "Mom?"

"And Dad." He waved to the man in the driver seat and leaned close to Jayne's ear. "They don't live close by."

His mother got out of the car and walked over, wearing a large smile. "Aren't you going to introduce us?"

"Mom, Dad, this is Jayne Warren. Jayne, these are my parents Alex and Mila. Jayne is—"

"I know who she is now." His mother extended her hand. "Irisa has told us so much about you."

"She speaks very highly of you." His dad also shook her hand. "How are you enjoying the tour?"

"It's been interesting."

"Why don't you both come to dinner tonight? I want to hear all about how the tour is going."

Zander shook his head. "Sorry, we can't."

She gaped at him. From the way he and Irisa spoke about family, she was surprised he'd turn down dinner. She was about to tell him not to worry about the sleepover when another thought dawned. Maybe he didn't want her around them. An uncomfortable feeling curled in her gut and she wrapped her arms around her middle. She'd give him an easy out if he needed one. "You know, you don't have to do that thing with me tonight. It's not a big deal. You can have dinner with your parents instead. I really should be getting settled with Patch one-on-one anyway."

He frowned at her, narrowing his gaze, then

turned to his parents. "We can't do dinner, but we can grab coffee now if you're free. There's a place about five minutes away. They have tables outside so we can bring the dogs."

Mila beamed. "We'll meet you there."

When they climbed into the car, Zander turned to her. "You're angry."

"No. I'm confused about why you turned down dinner with them. If you turned it down because of the whole sleepover thing, well, that could have been moved back later. And if you didn't want me at their house, I gave you an easy out so you could still go."

He rubbed his hands over his face. "I don't know if my sister ever mentioned that my mom's been on this babies and wedding kick for a few years now."

"And you don't want me getting any ideas?"

"Damn it, that's *not* what I'm worried about. Get as many ideas as you want." His eyes flashed at her in challenge. "She can be relentless and she's not subtle and I didn't want you to feel uncomfortable. She met Dom for the first time last week and told him and my sister they'd make pretty babies together. He rolled with it, but my sister freaked out. My mom doesn't have a filter when it comes to this."

"Oh."

He eased the car onto the road. "So now you know. Forewarned, forearmed, whatever. But no matter what happens, you're coming over tonight. You're sleeping in my bed. And Patch can get settled in with Shredder because they're going to be spending a lot of time together."

His harsh tone and the muscle jumping in his jaw told her the extent of his anger. He'd spoken to Luke that way, but never to her. She clasped her hand over her pendant—the one he'd given her. The heart pressed into her palm. She lowered her hand to her lap.

The car pulled into a parking space. His parents were seated at one of the coffee shop's tables.

Zander was out of the car and had both dog's leashes in hand by the time Jayne had finished unbuckling her seatbelt. His rigid posture and clenched jaw telegraphed his anger for anyone to see.

His parents greeted the dogs while Jayne took a seat. The small, square table insured she bumped knees with Zander. The heat in his eyes and the tension in his features hadn't faded.

They placed their orders. Zander all but growled his. Mila exchanged a look with Alex and murmured something in Ukrainian. Jayne only understood a handful of words, thanks to Irisa, and most of them were expletives or foods. Those wouldn't help her here.

Zander's head snapped up. He barked something back in his native tongue. Definitely sexy.

"Jayne, I love your hair. It's such a pretty shade."

She smiled at his mother. "Unfortunately, it's from a bottle. My real color is pale blonde."

"We've never had a blonde in the family."

Again, Zander spoke a few low, unfamiliar

words. The tone sounded threatening, but she couldn't know for sure.

"Do you come from a big family?" Undeterred, his mom continued.

"Not really. I'm an only child. My parents divorced when I was a teenager. They've both since remarried. I don't see them very often. We're not very close." Why couldn't her family be anything like his? She glanced down. Shredder nudged his head into her legs, then settled on her feet.

"Enough with the questions." Zander's hand met hers under the table. He still looked completely pissed off, but she no longer thought it was entirely on her.

His parents exchanged another look before his dad nodded and patted his mom's hand.

The waiter brought out their orders, including two bowls of water for the dogs. Everyone laughed over Patch's antics as he tried to share Shredder's bowl.

Alex asked Zander a few technical questions about the tour, drawing his son to less touchy topics.

Mila took his cue, asking about the band's travel and hotels. Jayne rattled off dates and flights and arrival times, and chatted about catering to the guys' specific needs.

"I'm so glad Zander has you to look after him." His mom smiled. "I've been telling him for a long time that he needs someone."

He set his cup down with a glare and a clatter.

Jayne risked another glance at her usually patient lover. "I'm just doing my job. But he's the easiest one to please. The least high-maintenance."

"Alex and I will be watching Shredder during the last two weeks of the tour. We'd be more than happy to watch Patch, too." Mila's gaze swung back and forth between Jayne and Zander.

Jayne tightened her hold on her mug. "That's very nice of you to offer, but I'm sure I'll figure something out."

"It's not a bother. And look at how well they're getting along. It wouldn't be good to separate them if they're spending a lot of time together. "

True, but now she had no idea how much time she and Zander would be spending together. "I'll think about it."

"Good." Mila signaled Alex and they stood. His mom gave her a hug. "We'd love to see you again, maybe you can come to the next family dinner. Hopefully, Zander will be in a better mood by then." She ruffled her son's hair before leaving.

He sat glaring into his coffee. "I warned them off questioning you."

"I gathered that much." She set her coffee aside. "What the hell? You made that so awkward."

"Me? I wasn't the one pumping out twenty questions."

"It wasn't twenty. She asked two."

"Thanks to my warning."

"I think it had more to do with your dad than you. Once he patted your mom's hand, she stopped." She dragged her hands through her hair and fought to control her emotions. "They have a relationship where all it takes is a pat on the hand to communicate what you're feeling. Anyone can tell by looking at them that they're still in love. You're lucky to have them."

He pushed away from the table. "I still don't want her scaring you off."

"You're doing that all on your own." She grabbed Patch's leash. "I'd appreciate it if you drive me home."

Fire-sparked hazel returned full-force. He palmed his keys. "Fine."

The blare of her cell phone made her jump. *Dalton's mom.*

"Hello?"

"Dalton ran away."

CHAPTER THIRTEEN

"What the hell? What does she mean, he ran away?" Zander grabbed his phone. No reply from Dalton to his earlier message. He sent another.

Jayne scrolled through her phone. "He came home from school, found out they were moving early and that Patch was gone, then he took off. He left a note saying he's been thinking about doing this for a while. A bunch of clothes are missing and he took his guitar."

"Did she check the community center?"

"She said she did. I just sent an email and a text to Kate."

He opened the car door and loaded the dogs in, then opened her door. "Get in. We're going hunting."

"We could cover more ground if you drop me off to get my car."

"Going in pairs is better."

They drove around for hours, didn't say much, and heavy silence lay over them like an awkward blanket. Finally, as sunset streaked colors across the sky, his phone rang. *Dalton.*

"It's him." He nudged Jayne's arm, and engaged the call. "Hey, bud."

"Um, I think I'm in trouble."

Shit. "Where are you?"

"I'm at a shelter but the guys here are bad news. It's going to be dark soon and I don't know where else to go."

"Which shelter? I'll come get you." He passed his phone to Jayne once he had the address. "Keep talking to him. He sounds scared."

Jayne kept up a running conversation about the dogs until they pulled up at the shelter.

Zander climbed out of the car, more worried than he'd wanted to let on. Anything could have happened to the kid.

Dalton hustled toward him, relief rushing across his features.

Thank God he was okay.

Jayne held back both Shredder and an excited Patch while Zander stowed Dalton's bag and guitar, and Dalton climbed into the backseat. Patch wriggled and whined until she let go of his leash. He leapt into Dalton's lap. He hugged Patch and kept his face buried in the dog's fur.

Zander couldn't just drop the kid off at home. Dalton wasn't ready and might run off again. "Did you eat dinner?"

"No."

"Okay then." He headed toward his house. Beside him, Jayne sent a text to Dalton's mom.

When they arrived, and the dogs raced around the yard, Jayne turned to them. "I'll start dinner. You guys relax."

Zander nodded his thanks. "Dalton, come on, let's sit out here for a while."

They sat by the pool. He kept his attention on

the kid, waiting until Dalton had calmed. "Why did you take off?"

"I'm losing everything—my house, my dog, the community center, my friends there, you."

"Why would you think you're losing me?"

"Because when I move, it'll be too far for me to get to the center. You're supposed to give me lessons at the center once the tour is over. I can't get my driver's license yet."

Zander hesitated to point out the how-to videos and phone calls the pair had exchanged over the last few weeks. Dalton knew about those. Maybe the real issue was he worried Zander would disappear from his life like everything else. "Do you think I've been spending time teaching you my solo just to stop in the middle?"

"Uh… No?"

"No. Tell me, do remember that big thing with wheels that we drove in today? I'll bet it would even take me to wherever you're moving."

"You'd really do that?"

"Again, I haven't been teaching you my solo for nothing."

"Wow." His voice cracked and he turned his face away. His breath hitched and his shoulders shook.

Zander leaned against his chair, giving Dalton a chance to deal with his emotions. He patted the kid's back. He'd never had anyone depend on him, but it felt damn good to be making a difference. "You can't run away anymore."

Dalton shrugged. "Not like anyone cares."

"If no one cared, your mom wouldn't have

called frantic and scared. If no one cared, would we have gone out looking for you? If no one cared, would I be here? Would Jayne be cooking you dinner? Would you be hanging out in my house? Would countless people at the center and your school have gone out searching?"

Dalton shrugged again. "I guess not."

"You guess right."

"I screwed up pretty big."

"You freaked out a lot of people, so yeah, you did. But I get it. Look, your situation stinks, but you're not alone. Your parents actually do care, but they're going through some pretty heavy stuff right now. Jayne went through what you're going through, I'm sure she'd talk to you about it if you want. How do you think she learned to play the piano? She lost herself in music when her parents' fighting got too bad."

"I didn't know that." He scuffed his sneaker against the patio. "I guess I could talk to her sometime."

"You should. And she's already told you that you can visit Patch whenever you want, and that he's yours no matter what."

"She's awesome."

"She is. If you can keep yourself together, you can help out backstage at shows. You'll learn a lot by shadowing Chad. And you know I don't let just anyone handle my guitars."

"You serious?"

"Yes." Zander reached over and ruffled Dalton's hair. "But if you run away again, I'll cut all of your guitar strings."

"Deal." Dalton hugged him tight.

Zander patted the kid's back. Jayne stood in the doorway, watching them with a big smile where a worry line used to be. He held out his hand toward her. He owed a lot to the incredible woman who'd put him in touch with the lonely boy. But most of all, he owed her an apology.

Jayne padded toward them. She slipped her hand in his and placed her other hand on Dalton's shoulder. Zander held tight to her delicate fingers. They remained joined together until the dogs came barreling in, demanding attention.

Zander showed Dalton where to wash up, then returned to the kitchen. Jayne set the table and chatted to the dogs sprawled exhausted on the floor.

He cleared his throat. "I'm sorry about this afternoon. You were right to call me out on it. I didn't want them to get in the way and push you out."

"I like your parents. They're fun." She placed her hand over his. "At least they care about you, and your mom is going out of her way to try to make sure you're happy. You saw what happened when you met mine. I'm more of an afterthought with them."

"I noticed that about your parents and I'm sorry. But you're not an afterthought with me. You know that, right?"

She squeezed his hand. "I do."

"So we're okay?"

She nodded. "By the way, those things you said in Ukrainian?"

"Yeah?"

"That was pretty sexy."

He met her gaze with a half-smile and raised a brow. "So, sleepover?"

"Sleepover." She laughed and the relaxed tone flowed over him. "But I have the feeling we won't be doing a lot of sleeping."

CHAPTER FOURTEEN

Jayne sat at Zander's kitchen counter, sipping chai tea and flipping through a magazine. Patch slept on the floor by her chair. Her cell phone rang, jarring a grumble out of the dog. Luke's name appeared on the display. She hadn't seen that in weeks. He hadn't bothered her, had only ignored her. Maybe he was trying to reach Zander. He was holed up in the practice room, finishing up a video chat guitar lesson with Dalton.

"Hello?"

"Yeah, I need tea for tonight."

No greeting. She shouldn't have expected on. She glanced at the clock on the wall. It was early. Several hours earlier than when he'd requested things before. "What kind?"

"There's a tea shop in San Diego. They have a special throat coat tea."

She did the quick calculation. "That's a three hour drive each way."

"So? I'm calling you early enough to account for that."

"No. We have that radio session this afternoon, remember? I'm going to that too."

"You can skip that. You're not needed there."

"But Zander wants me there. Even if he didn't,

this falls under the ridiculous demands category. There are plenty of throat-soothing teas that I'll be more than happy to get for you at any local store. I'm not driving for six hours."

"Please."

The word gave her pause. As did his tone. He'd never uttered that word to her. Not once. No *thank you*, either. And certainly not in almost-desperation. Something wasn't right.

"Look. You're obviously trying to get rid of me for most of the day. Not happening. I can call the shop in San Diego and have the tea delivered to your door by private service in three hours instead of me driving six."

More and more of their encounters and his cold stares and harsh glares came to mind. All of the stupid errands. All of the times he'd flat-out ignored her. And all the times she'd try thinking the best of him only to be disappointed again. "You look at me like you hate me. I've seen how you act with the guys, with the fans, and with Irisa, and I know you're not the asshole with them that you are with me. I'm sorry if I did something to make you hate me, but I've racked my brains trying to figure out what that could be, and I don't have any idea. What did I do?"

Silence. He hadn't hung up because his breathing came through the line.

He didn't answer, didn't care enough to answer. "Fine. If you want that tea, you can call the shop yourself to make arrangements. But don't ever bother me for anything again."

She ended the call and realized her hands were

shaking.

Irisa would need to know, and Luke might even be calling her now to complain. Her phone rang again. *Irisa.*

A deep breath didn't help her calm down. "Irisa. Hi. I was just about to call you."

"What's wrong?"

"Did Luke call you?"

"No. Why?"

Her heart pounded in steady, hard beats. "I'm finished with doing his ridiculous errands. I don't mind helping out the guys, but when he calls me and demands that I spend six hours driving to get him specialty tea, I put my foot down. He's not even nice to me anyway, no matter what I do. No band member has ever treated me this way. I'm done."

"Please don't quit. I need you. I didn't know what was going on."

She blinked at the distress in Irisa's voice. "I won't quit. I wouldn't do that to you."

"I'll talk to him. I promise."

No need to now, she'd told him off. But she knew her friend. Irisa would say something to him anyway. "Thanks. I don't want to put you in an awkward spot, but I'm sure he'll call you too, and I don't want you to think I'm not doing my job. I've put up with this stuff for weeks." Tension eased and she remembered Irisa had called *her*, not the other way around. "But that's not why you called me. What's up?"

"I was going to ask if you could go to the band's interview at KRIL this afternoon. I can't be there; something came up. But if you don't want to be near Luke, you don't have to go. The guys can do things on their own."

"I'll go. Zander already asked me, anyway. He mentioned they would be performing the new song he wrote." No way would she miss out on it this time.

Irisa let out a small sigh. "Thanks. I'll let you get back to your day. See you tonight at the show."

Jayne set her phone down. Her stomach ached. The thought of seeing Luke in a few hours was like preparing for battle.

Footsteps sounded behind her. "What did he ask you to do? I came in on the 'I've put up with this stuff for weeks' part."

She turned and faced Zander. A scary scowl darkened his face. "He asked me to drive to a shop in San Diego for tea."

"Are you fucking kidding me?"

"I didn't think to ask him that, but I'm sure he wasn't kidding."

"I'll rip his head off."

She placed her palms on his biceps. "It's okay. I flat out told him no."

He cupped her cheek. "Then why do you look like you're ready to cry?"

"Because I asked him why he treated me like I was worthless."

"Jayne—"

"I asked what I had done—what slight or insult or oversight that I unintentionally did to make him be such a jerk." Heat radiated off her face and her heart pattered hard.

"Honey. Calm down."

"And you know what he said?" She didn't give him a chance to respond. "Nothing. Absolutely nothing. What a—"

"Jayne," Murmuring her name, Zander gathered her close.

She hugged him back, cheek pressed into his shoulder.

His deep voice rumbled in his chest. "It's not you."

CHAPTER FIFTEEN

Zander pounded his fist into his legs, getting angrier and angrier with each passing minute. Brendan, Landry, and Jayne sat with him in the radio station's studio. They were waiting on Luke. And Luke was late.

An intern showed the members of Assertive Ire into the room. Griffin, Ben, and Tyler, but no Seth. Odd.

Zander leaned across an empty chair toward Griffin. "Where's Seth?"

"He's not answering his phone." At Griffin's hushed, serious response, a bad feeling formed in the pit of his stomach.

"Luke isn't either."

The DJ came in, downing coffee. "We're still waiting on Luke and Seth?"

"Maybe they're coming in together. Probably stuck in traffic." Brendan's suggestion could happen. Luke and Seth were good friends.

"All right. Well, shall we get on with the interview? Hopefully they'll arrive before your performance." He settled behind his desk. "We're coming back in ten seconds. Put on your headphones so we can take some calls."

Zander pulled on the bulky headphones and

glanced at his phone again. Nothing from Luke.

The DJ began, "And welcome back to The Afternoon Jungle. We're here with The Fury and Assertive Ire, co-headliners for the hottest ticket this summer. To start things off, we're giving you a chance to speak to the guys. Ask them anything you want." He rattled off the station's phone number. "We already have a bunch of callers lined up, so let's get right to them."

He looked at the bands. "Are you guys ready?"

"Sure." Zander nodded.

"Let's do it," Griffin agreed.

"John in Los Angeles, how's it going?"

"Hey man. Love your show. And I love The Fury. I'm at The Caboose right now and I think I found your missing member. Luke Thompson is here."

Oh no. Zander closed his eyes. Please be wrong.

"Well, put him on." The DJ gave Zander a thumbs-up.

"Yeah, I'm here." Luke's voice slurred. "Who's this?"

"This is KRIL. Your band The Fury is here with Assertive Ire giving an interview."

"Oh yeah, that's right. You know, I have some things I'd like to say about The Fury…"

The DJ grinned. "Well, sir, the floor is yours."

Zander pushed to his feet. "Shit. No way. Get him off the air."

"He has a right to speak."

Luke launched into a tirade about unsatisfactory help, Brendan's gummy bear attacks, and Zander's ballad. Then he said Jayne's name.

Zander's gaze shot to her.

Face red, her blue eyes met his—wide and panicked. Her hands gripped her headset. She mouthed, *Make it stop.*

"Get him the hell off the air." Zander ripped off his headset and slammed his fists on the DJ's desk. "Now."

Luke's angry voice continued, "I don't need any of you... My friend Seth was more than happy to give me a ride to The Caboose."

The DJ's laughter mingled with the sounds of the bar. "Classic rock and roll, man. What're you drinking?"

"Shit." Griffin stood up fast. "Seth can't be in a place like that. What's the address?"

"I have directions. I'm going to kill my brother." Ben, Assertive Ire's guitarist and Seth's brother, joined him. They ran out of the room with Tyler close behind.

Zander grabbed hold of the DJ's shirt collar. "I'm not kidding, man. End it, or I'll end you."

"No way. This is gold."

Shit. He tightened his hold, digging the fabric into skin. "I'm not kidding."

Face turning red, he nodded and ended the call. "So, that's what's new from Fury. We'll have a live studio session after this commercial break."

Zander shook his head. He expected them to perform after that? "Fuck that. We're leaving now."

He and Jayne rushed down the hall with Brendan and Landry close behind. They took off for their cars.

Zander slammed the car door behind Jayne. Missed calls and texts from Irisa lit up his phone. "Irisa's on her way to the bar. She'll probably get there first."

Fury pulsed with every heartbeat. He squeezed the steering wheel and floored the accelerator.

A crowd waited on the sidewalk outside the bar. When he and his band mates and Assertive Ire stepped onto the pavement, they erupted in shouts and cheers.

Zander grabbed hold of Jayne's hand and forged a path through the crowd to the door.

People stepped back, clearing the way to the bar. At the end, Luke stood, arguing with Irisa and Dom. Then Dom's arms circled Irisa's waist and he pulled her away to the other side of the room. Ready for a fight, Zander stormed over.

Luke glared at him. "What the hell do you want?"

Zander stepped forward until they were nose to nose. "We're gonna talk, you and me."

"Get the fuck out of my space." Luke shrugged away.

The bands' voices all mixed together, yelling over one another. Ben pushed forward and grabbed Luke's arm. "Where the hell is my brother?"

"I don't know, man."

A female scream pierced the air. "Seth's not breathing! I need an ambulance!"

Griffin, Ben, and Tyler took off for the back of the room. The woman screamed again. The crowd swarmed in all directions.

Zander stepped in front of Luke again. "What

the fuck were you thinking going on air like that, saying what you said?"

Luke pushed him back a step. "What's going on with Seth?"

"Someone here is an EMT. They're working on him." Jayne shouted over the crowd.

"You're the last person I expected to see here." Luke towered over her. "You're the last person I want to see here."

Zander guided her to the side, and then shoved Luke hard in the chest. "Watch yourself around her. She's my number one priority. You touch her, you hurt her in any way and we're done. She's in my life now, like it or not, and if you want to be too, then you'd better adjust fast. I know what you asked her to do today. What the fuck is your problem?"

"Screw you."

Sirens wailed in deafening volume, and then blue and red flashing lights illuminated the bar. The crowd scattered under the police officers' directions, making way for the paramedics. Zander pushed away from Luke. The paramedics loaded Seth onto a stretcher and rushed him out to the ambulance. Faces grim, Griffin, Tyler, and Ben followed.

Watching Seth being wheeled out, Zander felt helpless and angry. In need of comfort, he wrapped his arm around Jayne. An officer approached them. "Tell me what happened."

He and Jayne relayed their story about arriving at the bar, then Irisa and Dom joined them. In the corner of his vision, Luke gave his statement.

Behind them, Jake finished giving his.

Zander leaned down to Jayne's ear, murmuring

they needed to speak with Jake. He kept his arm around her and moved toward the man who had always been one of their biggest supporters.

"Jake, I'm sorry."

"I don't know what the hell happened. First Luke's drinking in here, then a mob shows up, then your band and Assertive Ire show up, then the whole place explodes. And Seth bringing drugs into my place? Not cool."

"I agree. Not cool at all. Bill me for all of the damages."

"I'll do that. Thanks."

"We wouldn't have gotten to where we are now without your support in the beginning. Whatever you need, man. Again, from the band, we're sorry."

Jake clapped him on the back and then walked away. Zander turned and faced his band mates standing twenty feet away in a pool of debris. They'd hit rock bottom. Squeezing Jayne's shoulder was the only thing keeping him from pounding his fist into Luke's face.

Luke stormed out of the building.

Holding onto Jayne, Zander returned to the group. "I told Jake to bill me for all damages."

Ringing echoed from Irisa's purse. She pulled out her phone. *Oliver Somers*. "Great. Just what I need."

Dom drew her closer. "I'd be happy to answer it for you."

"Me too." Zander snatched the phone from her hand. "Oliver, it's Zander. Irisa's busy right now. What do you want?"

"Zander," Oliver sputtered. "I saw pictures of

you guys. What's going on?"

Unbelievable. The meddling idiot. He shook his head at the group and banged his fist on the wall. "My band is fine. Griffin's is not. They're at the hospital with Seth and won't be playing tonight. You might want to be a little more concerned about them. We're on our way to sound check and it's on your head if we're late." He tapped the phone's screen to end the call, then held it out to his sister. "Done. Now let's get the hell out of here."

"Thank you." She stepped closer to Dom as his phone buzzed.

Zander nodded at them and then walked toward the exit. "Where the hell was Luke going?"

"He's stopping by the hospital on the way to the arena." Brendan kept pace beside him.

"If he doesn't show up..." He stopped walking. "I'm not kidding this time. If he doesn't show up, he's out of the band. I'm done dealing with him."

Landry looked at Jayne. "Luke had some interesting things to say about you."

She grasped her pendant. "I don't know why he doesn't like me."

"That seems to be his biggest problem." The bassist shook his head. "Makes me wonder..."

"Look." Zander slid his arm around Jayne. "If Luke has a problem with Jayne, then he has a problem with me. And if Luke has a problem with me, then he'd better be ready because we're going to deal with it once and for all."

***

An empty feeling weighed Jayne down. The arena was alive with sound but she couldn't muster any energy or spark. None of the band could. After everything that had happened that afternoon, the concert itself almost seemed silly. Who cared about a show when a man was fighting for his life and the members of her band were tearing each other apart?

Luke arrived and the tension in the room increased by a thousand percent. He walked by her, looking through her, not making eye contact, not acknowledging her any way at all. Zander observed, and followed Luke. They exchanged words and glares about something she was too far away to hear.

Tears prickled the backs of her eyes. She ducked into the restroom to calm down. She blamed herself for Zander and Luke's relationship plummeting—all the times Luke had been unkind to her, and the extra tension she'd caused between him and Zander. Too much had been said. The band looked on the verge of a breakup.

She couldn't allow it to happen.

She needed to find Irisa.

When she came out of the restroom, Irisa walked in her direction. Jayne took a deep breath. She wrung her hands together. "Can I talk to you?"

Irisa's eyes widened. "What's wrong?"

"I can't do this anymore. There's too much discord."

"You're quitting?"

"With other bands, I have to deal with some of the same issues, but it's not as bad. For whatever reason, Luke hates me."

"He doesn't hate—"

"He does. And for whatever reason, it's messing with the band's dynamic."

Irisa reached for her hand. "We need you."

"I need you as a friend more. If I stay, there won't be a band to manage. You need an effective assistant who doesn't make the band mates crazy. I can't give you that. You're my friend, and I care about your brother. I want this band to be successful. That's why I have to go."

"Have you talked to Zander?"

Her insides shook at the thought of having that conversation. "Not yet. You hired me, so I wanted to come to you first."

Irisa nodded. "I know you're right. I just didn't want it that way." She looked as exhausted as Jayne felt. "I'll tell him after the show."

"I'm sorry." In trying to save the band, she was letting down her best friend.

"Me too." A tight smile formed on her lips. "You might as well go on home now. Get a start on recovering from our craziness."

Jayne glanced toward the hallway leading to the exit. "I don't want to leave you hanging."

"Everyone's pretty emotional today. It's better that you go now."

"All right." Blinking back tears, she walked down the hall. And realized Zander had driven her to the venue. She rounded the building, heading to the cab station.

Gray, overcast skies settled a gloomy mask over the city. Tears burned her eyes. Biting her lip couldn't hold them at bay. Drawing deep breaths, she wiped at her cheeks.

Footsteps pounded the pavement. Zander stood in front of her, seething. "You quit?"

"I had to do it. Luke is too much of a live wire around me."

"Screw him. I need you."

"What happens on your next tour, or when you're back in town next month? Luke hates me. He'll tear you guys apart to prove it and I refuse to be the reason the band beaks up. You've worked so hard for so long. I won't do anything to hurt your success."

"None of that matters."

"Of course it matters. The band has always come first. It has to."

"Things change."

"Those guys have been part of your life a lot longer than I have. You have a responsibility to them, too."

"Bullshit."

She loved Zander, but she needed to be clear. "This thing with you and me—it can't work."

"So we're done? Just like that?" He turned and kicked a soda can clear across the street. It landed with a clatter.

She blinked hard, but the tears spilled down her cheeks. "You'll have a group of women waiting outside for you after tonight's show. You don't need me."

"You really fucking believe I can replace you?" He stared at her.

Her stomach churned. "Please. I don't know how to make this easy. On either of us."

"It's not easy. And you're wrong if you think I'm getting the hell out of your way."

"I don't want to break up the band. I won't have that hanging over me."

"But you'll walk out on what we have. You don't mind that hanging over you?"

Her heart broke at his words. He had no idea how badly she ached. "I'm doing this for you."

"Then stay. You staying with me is for my good. If you walk away, it'll wreck me."

"Not as much as staying and watching you and Luke ripping each other apart will wreck me. You've been friends for fifteen years. You've known me for two months."

"I'm in love with you."

Breath locked in her lungs. "What?"

He moved closer. "I'm in love with you."

Rational arguments slipped out of her head. He loved her.

"You mean more to me than anything. If I have to choose between you and my band, I'm choosing you."

"You can't."

"I'd rather walk away from them than lose you."

"Walking away isn't the answer. They need you. Dalton needs you. The community center needs you. As The Fury you guys do so much good for so many people. And you guys need each other. You can't lose all of that because of me. I won't let you choose me over them."

His phone vibrated. She glanced at her watch. "You're supposed to be on stage now."

"Fuck that. They can wait."

A cab pulled up to the curb. Clasping her heart pendant, she ducked around Zander. "If you really do love me, you'll get on that stage and make your fans happy."

He followed her. "Wait."

She climbed inside the car. If this was it, he might as well know the truth. "For what it's worth, I love you too."

CHAPTER SIXTEEN

She loved him too. Zander grabbed hold of the cab door. "We're not done."

A car behind them honked. The cabbie glanced over his shoulder. "Hey man, are you getting in or not? If not, you gotta get away from my door."

"Fine. Jayne, I'll come by tonight after the show."

"No. You can't. Staying apart is what's best for both of us." She closed the door and the cab zoomed onto the street.

The skies opened. Rain fell in large splotches. The sidewalks emptied as people hurried for cover. He stood staring at the cab as it grew smaller and smaller, a yellow dot disappearing into the horizon, leaving him in a world of cold and gray.

Luke was the reason. As the rain cooled his skin, rage heated his muscles, poking the fire, unleashing the beast.

This ended now.

Stalking through the halls, he made his way to the stage. His sister stood in his place, gripping his guitar. He held out his hand. "Give me that before you hurt someone."

Irisa handed it over. "Are you all right?"

He strapped on the guitar. "No. But I'll play.

You'd better go. This place is about to explode."

They opened with "Temperature Rising", then rolled into "Cut Down". While Luke talked to the crowd, Zander kept to his side of the stage. Anger simmered and he replayed the conversation with Jayne over and over. Her tear-stained face, the quaver in her voice, the gut-punching words. He wasn't going to lose her just because his band mate was an asshole.

He played the opening riff of "My Fist, Your Face." The heavy, volatile song, matched his mood perfectly. Zander moved closer to the fans, ready for his guitar solo that followed the last chorus. But instead of backing away from the front of the stage when the solo began, Luke kept singing, improvising lyrics and stealing the spotlight. His fuck-you glare when he met Zander's gaze set off the spark waiting to ignite.

Zander kicked him and glared, playing even faster. Luke's fist slammed into his shoulder and the asshole kept singing. Zander swung his guitar behind him and then shoved at Luke's chest with both hands. The singer stumbled backward a few steps. Damn, that felt good. The drum beat and Landry's guitar fell silent.

"What's with you? Have a fight with your girlfriend?" Eyes flashing blue fire, Luke lunged at Zander with a punch.

He ducked and countered with his own. "Fuck you. She left me because of you, asshole."

The drums resumed, and fueled Zander's punches with a rapid-fire melody.

Hands pulled on his shoulder, separating him

from Luke. Landry shoved in between them. "What the fuck, guys? Stop. You're not doing this now."

Breathing hard, Zander glanced at the bass player, then at Luke, and finally at the crowd. He'd never lost control on stage. But then again, he'd never lost anything as important as Jayne.

Landry pushed Luke toward the left side of the stage, then pointed Zander to the right side. "Stay the hell away from each other until the show's over."

He grabbed the mic and said something that made the crowd cheer. Zander couldn't make out the words over the blood rushing in his head. He slipped his guitar strap over his head and launched into the next song.

Landry stayed in the middle of the stage for the rest of the show. Whenever he turned toward Zander, he shook his head—disapproving, angry, and ready to fight.

As soon as the show ended, Zander grabbed hold of Luke's shoulder. "Right now. You and me. The dressing room."

Luke shoved away. "Fine."

Zander looked over his shoulder at Irisa, Landry, Brendan, and the crew. "No one else comes in."

He followed Luke and then slammed the door at his back. "What the fuck is your problem with Jayne?"

"Forget it."

"No. She *left* me because of you. She said she wouldn't stay and be the reason the band breaks up. She wouldn't let me choose her over you because she thinks our friendship means too much to me. But you know something? It doesn't. *Nothing* means more to me than her. So you'll answer my fucking question or we're done as of right now and the band can be fucking finished too. I don't care anymore. So, I'll ask again, what is your problem? Why do you care if I'm in love with Jayne? Do you want her? Is that it?"

"Fuck. No." Luke paced the room like a caged tiger. Restless and ready to pounce. "It's Audrey."

Zander frowned, searching his brain until the name clicked. The clothing designer who'd helped out on their last few East Coast tours. He'd suspected something brewing between Luke and Audrey, but when the band left New York, Luke hadn't mentioned her again. "That still doesn't explain why you've been a class-A dick to Jayne."

"She doesn't look a damn thing like Audrey, but the way she talks and moves is the same. And that gold pendant she was wearing every day is one of Audrey's designs. Every time she touched it, it hurt me. And the way she sneaks looks at you—like Audrey used to do at me. Being around her is hard. I couldn't deal so I'd leave, but if I couldn't get away, then I sent her on errands to keep her away from me. I guess I hoped she'd get tired of it and quit."

"Are you fucking serious?"

"I'm not proud of it, but yeah."

Rage fired his blood. How could Luke be so self-absorbed? And so damn mean? He'd lost Jayne all because Luke was acting like nothing more than a teenager. Well, they were through. His whole life trashed. He grabbed his guitar by the neck and swung it over his head.

An unexpected force caught and prevented him from slamming it into the concrete floor. He tugged again, but it was yanked out of his hands. He whirled around.

Luke held the blue Gibson in a protective hug. "You can't break this, man."

"Why? Does the band really matter to you?"

"Of course it does."

Seething, he shoved a chair out of the way. "I should rip your fucking head off. Do you know what you put Jayne through?"

"Yeah. I'm sorry. I was being an asshole. I wasn't thinking clearly." Voice calmer, he paused and for the first time, Zander saw the pain in his eyes. And actual contrition. "She's engaged now, you know. Audrey, I mean."

"Is she?"

Luke nodded. "To some New York suit. Found out about that today. Found out she was seeing him the same day we met Jayne."

"The day you were arrested. Damn it. You should've said something when we hired her."

"What the fuck was I supposed to do? Cry and talk about my *feelings*?" He snarled the word, lip curling as though he'd tasted something sour.

"Maybe if you'd talked more about them, Audrey wouldn't be engaged to that suit." Expecting the punch, Zander braced and then countered with his own hold. "And, Jayne wouldn't have had the worst experience of her life."

Luke slowly shook his head and backed away.

"I know I fucked up."

"You better sort out your shit over Audrey because I'm not letting Jayne go. If you can't, then this tour is it for me and The Fury can find another guitarist. Or, I really will kick you the hell out of the band." And the blue guitar would no longer matter.

"Understood." Luke rubbed his forehead. A stab of sympathy welled in Zander's chest. They'd been friends for years, as close as brothers. He'd never seen Luke like this.

The door slammed open and Brendan and Landry pushed their way into the room. Brendan spoke first. "In case you forgot, we're part of this band, too. No one makes decisions about kicking people out without all the band weighing in, but as far as I'm concerned, both of you are on notice."

Landry nodded. "I'm getting really tired of the drama. This has been going on the entire tour. Your shoving match on stage tonight was the last straw."

"We're all a little burned out," Brendan added, "but you don't see Landry and me running our mouths or getting into fights."

"You will be in one if you throw one more goddamn gummy bear. This isn't just on Zander and me." Luke aligned himself by Zander's side.

Landry jumped to Brendan's defense. Battle lines were drawn, new grievances aired, and long-dead issues revived. The dressing room seemed small with all of their voices. Anger and frustration ran hot in Zander's blood, tempered only by guilt when a remark rang true. His band was a bleeding wound and he didn't have a clue how to stitch it back together.

"Stop!" The word exploded out of his sister.

They all turned toward her, the silence glaringly loud amid the pulsing emotions and absence of heated words.

Irisa stood in the middle of the room, hands clasped to her chest in entreaty. "Just stop. This isn't helping. You're friends. Remember that before you say anything else."

Her pale face and wounded eyes cut through his frustration at his band mates. "What's going on? You look like you're about to fall over." Now that he knew about the antacids, he couldn't stop worrying about her. He covered the distance between them in quick strides.

"I just spoke with Oliver. Excite is demanding that I resign as your manager, effective immediately."

"What?"

"They've put a lot of money into you, and given recent events, they feel that I'm incapable of keeping things together." She glanced at each of them. "And after what I witnessed tonight, they're right."

"Screw them. You're my sister. They can't make you quit." The familiar burn of anger tingled in his blood. Oliver was an asshole.

Her shoulders sagged. "If I don't resign, they're going to pull you guys off the tour."

Pulled off? The notion was insane. He shook his head. "They wouldn't kick us off."

"Is it so hard to believe? Not to me. Not after all that's happened since before it began. The arrest, the bar fight, Luke quitting, Luke and Zander's behavior during the interview, the disaster at the bar, the mess with Jayne, and now a fistfight on stage." She ticked off each instance on her fingers. "I've failed at keeping things calm. Maybe you do need someone else."

"No way. I lost Jayne today. I'm not losing you, too."

"The alternative is getting pulled from the tour. You don't want that. I don't want that."

"It's always been family-first with us, right? That's not changing now." He spoke the words he'd thought his sister wanted to hear and exchanged glances with each of the guys. They were like brothers to him. He missed the closeness, the support, the us-against-the-world bond they'd shared before ego and exhaustion had taken hold. "Maybe we lost focus of that."

For a long moment, no one moved or offered any encouragement. Maybe they were too broken to mend. The thought gutted him as much as losing Jayne had.

Brendan moved first. He and Landry had every right to want to walk away. Instead, he met Irisa's gaze. "We wouldn't be the same without you. The band needs you, Irisa." The tentative smile aimed at Zander spoke volumes. "The band needs all of us."

Relieved, Zander clapped him on the back. "Thanks, man."

Hands tucked in his back pockets, Landry strolled over and stood next to Brendan. "No one else would fit." His comment seemed to be addressed both to Irisa and to Zander. Hopefully, he meant it.

Two down, one to go. Zander looked at Luke. Resentment still festered over what happened with Jayne. If Luke joined them, things would have to change because Zander was determined to win her back. But right now, he needed everyone on board to back up his sister.

The ever-present scowl finally missing, Luke joined them. He touched Irisa's shoulder. "You're as much a part of this band as we are."

The breath he'd been holding released. It wasn't too late, they still had a shot. For the first time in a long time hope enveloped him like a balm.

Irisa's gaze jumped between the guys. "You've been at each other's throats, but my problem makes you all come together?"

Zander rested his hand on Luke's shoulder, then nodded toward Brendan and Landry. "We cleared the air on a few things while you were on the phone."

"I walked in on the tail end of that conversation, remember? It wasn't friendly."

"No. Before that..." He raised his eyebrows at Luke. He hated to make the guy relive his pain, but no way would he be the one to share Luke's story.

The singer nodded. "What happened with Seth was a wake-up call. He went in the back room, and I was so ticked off and caught up in the interview I didn't realize he never came out. I lost focus and blame myself for him ending up in the hospital. I've already apologized to Griffin and his band, and to these guys, but I need to apologize to you. I've been an asshole for a while. I'm sorry."

"*Why* have you been one?"

Luke shoved his hand through his hair. "Audrey Pierce."

A line formed between his sister's brows. "I don't understand."

"I thought we had something, but she had other thoughts…" He glanced at Zander, then shifted back to Irisa. "When Jayne laid into me today about not running that errand, some things she said really hit home. I figured out of all people, I could talk to you about it, and about Audrey, so I called you…"

"And I bit your head off and didn't even listen to you." Eyes widened, she reached for him, but then pulled her hands back into her lap.

He shoved his hands in his pockets and shrugged. "Seth stopped by after that and suggested we go to the bar to cool off before the interview, but as I sat there, I got angrier and angrier, and, well, you know what happened then."

"I'm sorry I wasn't there for you. It won't happen again." She grasped his hand.

A stormy sea of emotions swept across his face. "I know it hasn't seemed like it, but I don't want to hurt the band."

"We're good now, man." Landry patted him on the back. "We yell, we fight, we throw punches, then it's over and done, until the next one."

She pressed her lips together and regarded them for another moment. "If I stay, what if Excite makes good on their threat to pull you?"

Getting kicked off a tour wasn't unheard of, regardless of the size and popularity of the band. Zander smirked to cover the sudden unease skating through his system. "Do you know how much money they'd risk losing if they did that?"

Luke nodded at him. "I say we call their bluff."

After all that had happened, and the guys agreeing to stick together and support his sister, he couldn't have their tour snatched away. He'd fight with everything he had before he'd allow that to happen.

His sister rose to her feet. "So what do we do?"

"We storm the castle, together." And maybe they'd be able to heal the damage to their bond.

"You mean show up at Excite? I hate the idea of throwing myself on Oliver's mercy, especially face to face." Irisa's features twisted like she'd downed a shot of bad-tasting medicine.

Zander touched her arm. He'd get rid of Oliver. "You're not asking that jerk for anything. We're going to the top. We're flying to Vance's house in Vegas." Vance DuBrow, Excite's president, would see them even if Zander had to beat down the old man's door. No one made threats to his sister.

"Now? It's eleven thirty."

"Threatening to pull us off the tour was a stupid move, and he's going to see how much." Zander grabbed his phone, hoping to see a text or call from Jayne. Nothing. "I'll make the reservations for the flight and text you. Go home and pack a bag. Get some sleep, or hell, come over and crash at my place. We'll leave from my house in the morning."

"This is crazy. We're going to show up at his home on a Sunday, uninvited?"

"He asked for it. Let's get out of here." Zander led the way toward the exit. The Fury was *his* band.

No one else would tell them they were done.

CHAPTER SEVENTEEN

The guys had taken him up on his offer. Luke sprawled on his couch, Brendan sat on the floor with Shredder, tapping beats against the coffee table, and Landry lounged in his recliner. They were laughing and joking, but more subdued than normal, polite and careful, like they were almost afraid to say something that could be taken the wrong way. Considering how long they'd had problems, he couldn't expect things to return to normal immediately, especially not with their careers hanging by a steel string.

At dawn, everyone piled into his car. He hadn't slept well at all. Jayne was being stubborn, ignoring his calls and texts. He'd been tempted to go to her place and break down the door, forcing her to listen to him, but that wouldn't have solved anything. She believed she was doing the right thing for him.

Damn it, *she* was the right thing for him. He had to make her understand.

All during the drive and the flight, his thoughts kept drifting back to Jayne but Irisa's continued silence puzzled him, as well. After arriving at his house the night before, she'd gone immediately to the guest room. He knew she was feigning sleep behind her dark sunglasses during their travels. When they climbed into the rental car in Vegas, he snatched the glasses off her face.

She made a grab for them. "Hey."

"What's wrong?" He held them away from her.

Brendan leaned forward in his seat. "You were too quiet during the trip. What's up?"

Her mouth tightened. "I told Dom I couldn't see him anymore."

"Why?" If he had to kick Torres' ass on top of everything else…

"Because the band needs my full focus. Everything that went wrong happened while I was distracted by my relationship with him."

Shock straightened his spine. "You're kidding, right? We were fighting before you got involved with him."

She shook her head. "But all the really bad stuff occurred afterward."

Luke lowered his sunglasses, blue eyes serious. "We're all adults. We're responsible for our own actions. None of the stupid things I or anyone else did were your fault."

"But I might have prevented disaster if I'd been paying more attention. I can't help feeling responsible. I could've prevented the bar fight. I would've gone to the interview."

"Can't guarantee that." Brendan, always the peacemaker, gave her a smile. "You could've been in the restroom when the first fight started, and you could've missed the interview if you'd been sick. No matter what you do, there's no way to make sure everything will be smooth. You're allowed to have a personal life."

Zander nodded. "You were happy with Dom. I'd rather see you happy than resenting us down the line because you missed out on something good with him."

"No. I need to make sure nothing else goes wrong. I need to be in my usual *all band, all the time* mode."

He handed over the sunglasses. "You were popping meds because of your *all band, all the time* mode. I was an idiot for not seeing it. Maybe I'm a perfectionist with music, and you are with, well, everything. But we all should've insisted on you sharing the workload, no matter how hard you fought to manage it all yourself."

"You guys have to handle the music and the fans, and you get so caught up in it and lose track of everything else... And Brendan's even worse with remembering about being on time for things, and Luke and Landry—"

Raising his brow, Landry held up his hand. "Luke and I aren't helpless. We're not as lost in our own world as Zander."

"Hey, I managed to handle the flight and car for this trip, didn't I?" Leaning forward, he cuffed the back of the bassist's head. "And I didn't say things would be perfect. If something gets messed up, it gets messed up. That's why you also need an assistant. Someone like Jayne who double-and triple-checks things." He glanced at Luke. Hurting his friend was the last thing he wanted to do. "But maybe not actually Jayne—not right now, anyway."

Luke turned toward the window. "Don't let me stand in the way. I'll deal with it…better than I did before."

He hoped so. Jayne mattered to him, more than anyone ever had. He loved her. Choosing between Jayne and his band would be painful, awful. He didn't want to lose them, but he couldn't lose her.

Irisa nudged Luke's shoulder. "Any news on Seth?"

He nodded. "Griffin texted me. Seth's awake, and going to do a lengthy rehab stay once he gets out of the hospital."

"I'm glad he's okay. Hopefully he'll get the help he needs." She patted his arm, then twisted toward Zander. "So what are we going to say to Vance, anyway?"

"Leave it to me." He rolled his shoulders as the massive estate came into view.

He'd been to Vance's house a few times before and had made friends with the security guard. After a few minutes of small talk, the guard waved them through. Vance had granted the all-clear for his biggest client. The son-of-a-bitch acted like he was king.

"Let me do the talking." Zander followed the guys out of the car. Together as a unit, they ascended the stone steps.

The front door swung open. Vance DuBrow stood before them. His slicked-back hair, tinted glasses perched low on his nose, and scowl were at odds with his colorful golf attire. "To what do I owe the honor of this visit?"

Zander took the older man's sneer with a nod

and crossed his arms over his chest. "When you have your lackey tell my sister that she needs to resign from being band manager or you're going to kick us off the tour, you can bet I'm going to have a problem with that."

Luke flanked Irisa's other side. "We all have a problem with that."

Vance gestured for them to come inside, and they crowded into the foyer. "I've always liked you guys, but lately you've been in the spotlight for the wrong reasons."

"Lately, we've had some extenuating circumstances." Landry stood shoulder to shoulder with Luke and Brendan stepped up beside Zander. Solid support and a united front.

After nodding at the drummer, Zander turned his gaze to their host. Money drove Vance's every decision. Channeling his anger, Zander aimed for the man's bank account. "Here's the thing, Vance. We're a package deal. My sister stays. I'm sure you thought about the money. If you kick us off, you can expect the fans to be pissed and for sales to fall. But if you're ready to do that, then we're ready to part ways completely."

"You can't walk away. You owe Excite one more album."

"Then throw together a greatest hits collection for all we care. You won't get any new music. If you're so ready to wash your hands of us..." He shrugged and let the threat hang in the air.

Lips pressed together, Vance stared at them for a long moment, stroking his chin.

Zander widened his stance, meeting old man's

stare with matching intensity. "I expect you to be straight with me. Have those extenuating situations you mentioned been cleared up?"

Zander glanced at the guys. They could pull off the rest of the tour. They nodded and his sister answered, "Yes."

"Do I have your word that nothing else will happen?"

Irisa stepped forward and Zander followed suit, ready to back her up. "You've known us for ten years. That should count for something."

Ten years. Too damn long for them to lose all they'd built up. Too damn long to let anything come between them. Yeah, they needed a break, but not a *break up*. Zander rolled his shoulders. One tour out of all those years couldn't sink them. Yeah, they'd been stupid. He didn't expect Vance to be sentimental. The man looked at the bottom line and money won out over anything else.

Vance gave them a slight nod. "All right. Then you can stay on the tour."

Half of the battle won... Zander raised his brow at Vance. "With Irisa."

"With Irisa," Vance confirmed.

Zander laid his hand on her shoulder. He'd promised to help ease her workload, and Vance had the power to remove one of her biggest headaches. "One more thing. I don't want us to have to deal with Oliver anymore."

"Why?"

"He oversteps a lot, and he makes my sister uncomfortable. I'm not okay with my sister being uncomfortable."

In the corner of his vision, his sister smiled and the tension in her shoulder eased.

"Fine. Done." Vance glanced at her, and then his gaze spanned the rest of the group. "Anything else?"

"We didn't eat on the plane." Brendan flashed a smile and Zander laughed. "I'm a little hungry."

Irisa stifled a groan. "Brendan, we're not making Vance feed us. We'll get something at the airport." She extended her hand to Vance. "Thank you."

He nodded and returned the shake. "I expect a decent report on the next show."

"You'll get one."

"Then get outta here and earn your pay. Your rock'n roll dramatics made me twenty minutes late for my tee off."

When they returned to the car, Irisa hugged him. "No more Oliver. I think that deserves its own celebration. Thank you for doing that for me. For the first time in years, I won't cringe when I deal with Excite."

"Hey, you look out for us, I'm just returning the favor. No one fucks with my family."

They arrived at the airport an hour before their flight. Zander and Luke grabbed coffee for the group while Irisa, Brendan, and Landry went looking for breakfast. After securing seats for the others, Zander settled into an uncomfortable chair across from Luke and stared at the steam rising from the cup in his hand.

He'd helped save his band. The guys were getting along much better. Things would have been perfect but he still didn't have Jayne.

Luke nudged Zander's chair with his boot. "Call her. Tell her to come back."

Zander swallowed a mouthful of coffee, then balanced the cup on his knee and regarded his friend. Luke looked like hell. "Are you really going to be okay with that?"

Slouched in his chair, legs kicked out in front of him, Luke nodded. "I'll deal with it, and I won't be an ass this time. She's important to you, and I don't want her hating me or refusing to see you because of me."

He'd never forget Jayne's teary-eyed, defeated expression. "She'll need a lot of convincing before she'd agree. If she even agrees."

A light sparked in Luke's eyes. "I have an idea."

CHAPTER EIGHTEEN

The community center was a flurry of activity. Jayne stood in the music room as old instruments were hauled away. The shipment Zander had promised Kate had arrived. Guitars, three drum kits, mics, amps, even a new piano. Her throat thickened when she touched the keys. He'd done that for her.

It looked like she'd have a lot more time for piano lessons. Vendetta's manager called to inform her that the band had canceled their summer tour. They were taking a break, citing artistic differences. Was every band she connected with doomed for failure?

Footage of The Fury's concert from the previous night had surfaced, and she couldn't get the image of Zander and Luke throwing punches on stage out of her head. She had to be the reason. The temptation to reach out to Zander was strong. Her phone held the two voicemails and texts he'd left. *Call me. I need to talk to you.* And, *Stop being stubborn and answer the phone. We can work this out. I need you.*

Torn between missing him and doing what was best for him, she didn't know what to do. And music, her lifeline, just reminded her of Zander and the mess with the band. Her reflection in the window caught her attention. Being a strawberry blonde had been fun, but she missed her platinum locks. *Change your look and change your life*. She'd tried that once, going for the red tint after Pepper had died. Life hadn't worked out well as a redhead.

Three hours later, after a trip to the salon, she was back to being blonde. And she couldn't get any blonder than the platinum locks. *Blondes have more fun.* She needed fun, but more than fun, she needed something to go *right*.

She sat at the piano, playing with a version of the song Zander had written. A knock at her door broke her concentration. She checked the peephole, blinked, then checked again, sure she was seeing things. Nope. He really was there. Trepidation rose like a ball in her stomach. Why was he there?

Only one way to tell. She flipped the locks and eased the door open.

Luke towered over her, for once not wearing his usual scowl. "Hi."

"How did you get in here?"

"Your neighbor held the security door open for me. Can I come in?"

Too many question swirled in her head. She nodded and stepped back. Patch, far from being a guard dog, ran to the bedroom.

He shoved his hands in his pockets. Then withdrew them and sighed. "Look, there's no easy way to say this. I was an asshole to you and I'm sorry."

"Um… Okay?" She frowned as he paced her living room.

Coming to a stop in front of her piano, he faced

her. "I won't be one anymore. I swear. Please come back on tour."

"Wait. What? Why would you of all people want me back?"

"One—Zander needs you. You mean a hell of a lot more to him than anything else. And, two— you're really good at your job. Irisa was headed for a breakdown and you saved her. The band needs you."

"But you don't like me. You're always so—"

"Awful? I know. I'm sorry. It was never anything personal against you." He shoved his hand through his hair. "You remind me of someone I lost. Seeing you every day was a continual reminder that I'd fucked up something special and lost it for good."

The pain in his eyes tugged at her. "I'm sorry."

A bitter laugh escaped his throat. "I don't deserve your forgiveness or your pity. I know that, believe me. But despite what you've seen, I'm not usually an asshole."

"I did notice that, actually." She eased her hip against the side of the couch. "I'd see these glimpses of kindness when you were with Irisa or Dalton and wonder what I did to make you hate me."

He touched the framed photo of Pepper on her desk. "It was never about you. I wish I could redo the last few months. There's a lot I'd change. A lot."

She knew the band had a show in Sacramento that night. "Do the guys know you're here?"

"They know. Zander and I had a long talk. We're fine now. Except for the part about you being here in L.A. and not up in Sacramento with us." He walked to her window showcasing her view of the mountains. "Zander's never brought someone on tour. I get that you were working with us and not some chick who tagged along, but it's still the same thing. He's never been so wrapped up in someone before. It's obvious you're special to him. He was ready to leave the band for you. It kills me knowing how much of a mess I made and that you were going to give him up."

"It was either that, or watch the band break up, and I couldn't do that to him, not after seeing how much you guys mean to each other."

He turned to face her. "I've seen the way you two act, how you are. You go out of your way to make sure we're happy. Zander does that for you too. You've been doing little things to take care of each other since day one the tour. Bottom line, you guys make each other better. You need each other. Don't throw that away. Not for anything."

She hugged herself. "I don't want to agree to come back and then have the same problems again."

"I swear it. Even if I have to duct tape my mouth shut." He smiled.

"Please be kidding. I don't know how you'd manage to sing that way."

He rubbed his hand over his face, his expression a combination of weariness, sadness, and loneliness. "I can't promise I'll be happy and cracking jokes all the time, but I know how bad I messed up before. You have my word that nothing else will happen. I'm dealing with my problem. You make my best friend happy. I'd like to think we'll be friends someday but I know it might take a while for you to trust me."

Hope stirred in her chest. "I'd like that."

"I do, too. So does this mean you're back with us?"

"What about the other guys and Irisa? I did bail on them. They may not want me back."

"This might convince you." He opened the door. Irisa, Brendan, and Landry crowded into the doorway. She didn't see Zander.

Irisa entered first and caught her in a hug. "I was so worried you'd hate me. Of course we want you back. The rest of the tour is going to be so much better, I promise."

When Irisa released her, a grinning Brendan hugged her. "Glad to have you back. My gummy bear stock is running low."

"But, it's only been a day since I refilled them."

He shrugged. "Things happen."

"He lost them to a kid at the airport." Landry was next in line, more subdued, but he gave her a smile. "But more important than that, welcome back."

She swallowed hard and turned toward the source of the drama. Blue eyes sober, Luke extended his hand. "Again, I'm sorry."

"Apology accepted." She placed her hand in his. A handshake equaled a promise. They'd start over with a blank slate. "Guys, where's Zander?"

"Behind you." Zander's voice filled the room.

Heart in her throat, she slowly turned.

A muscle worked hard in his jaw. He looked exhausted. "Welcome back."

She swallowed several times to hold back her

tears. "Zander."

He turned to his band. "I need to talk to Jayne alone."

One by one, they filed out of the room. Luke closed the door at his back.

"The blonde suits you." His gaze held hers. He treaded close enough for her to smell his scent, close enough for her to touch him but she resisted.

"I needed a change." She reached for her pendant and her hand closed over the heart he'd given her.

His stare shifted to her clasped hand holding his heart, then back to her face. "I need you back. Not just as tour manager. I need you by my side, in my life. I love you."

Her throat thickened. "I love you, too."

His hands dove into her hair and his mouth fused with hers. Jayne strained closer, winding her arms around his neck, then sliding one into his hair. His tongue licked along the seam of her lips. She opened for him, stroking the wet heat, angling for a deeper taste. She missed him. It didn't matter that they'd only had a short separation. In her heart it had felt as deep and wide as an ocean. His arms around her, his hands roaming along her back, his scent, his taste—all of that felt *right*. As necessary to life as oxygen or food.

"Missed you." He murmured the words between kisses trailed along her jaw.

"Me too." She tugged his shirt up and slipped her hands under the fabric. Warm skin, hard muscles, a fast-beating heart.

Knocking interrupted their reunion.

"Guys," Brendan's voice came through. "We're going to miss our flight. Save the make-up sex for when we get to the hotel in Sacramento."

Heat flushed into her cheeks. Jayne buried her face in Zander's neck. "Oh my God."

"Don't worry, I'll kill him." He pulled back and nudged her chin until her gaze met his. "And then we'll take up his suggestion when we get to the hotel."

Her body yearned for the welcoming heat and sensations of joining with his. "I think we should do that part first."

He groaned and pulled her tighter against him. "I like the way you think."

***

The arena buzzed with energy. Waiting in the wings, Zander felt it in his bones. Excitement, adrenaline, contentment, feelings swirled together in preparation for the final show of the tour. They were home, and closing out the tour in L.A. felt right. Everyone could sleep in their own beds tonight.

Jayne brushed by him, her hands full of t-shirts for the evening's giveaway. Having her back meant everything. He grabbed her around the waist and pulled her in for a kiss. "I can't wait until I get you alone in that hotel room tonight."

He'd booked a suite in a hotel close to the arena so they could begin celebrating the end of the tour as soon as possible. Plus, he wanted to spoil her with the five-star treatment she deserved.

"Break a leg out there. But don't break anything else. I have plans for you for later." She leaned into him for a moment before continuing on with her task.

Once Irisa had released her stranglehold on her duties, she and Jayne and the band had worked out a balance. More importantly, his sister had worked out her relationship with Dom. The sparkling diamond on her left hand glinted under the stage lights.

Beside him, Dalton shadowed Chad, watching as he tuned a guitar. The kid looked a hell of a lot happier than he'd been when Zander first met him. Dalton and a lot of the kids at the center would benefit from the band's donations of instruments, money, and time. He had gotten every member of the band on board to help out with lessons there, and had pledged to support the center with whatever they needed going forward. He finally felt like he was making a difference, and that was all thanks to Jayne.

Luke wandered over. "Are you going to do it tonight?"

He shook his head. The purchase Luke had accompanied him to buy that afternoon was safely hidden in his suitcase. "I had an idea for doing it when Jayne and I get home from the hotel tomorrow morning. Maybe you could help me out?"

"Whatever you need." He smiled and waited for Brendan and Landry to join them. "Ready to rock this place?"

He'd never looked forward to a performance more. "Let's do it."

Together, they took the stage, basking in the glow of lights, fans, and friendship.

CHAPTER NINETEEN

The next morning...

"Home. Finally." Zander drove his new Camaro through the gates of his estate. He rolled his shoulders and parked the car. He'd been operating on a buzz of anticipation for hours. Countless texts with Luke confirmed plans were set for his surprise. The tour was over and the rest of the summer stretched out before him. He pictured relaxed days, lots of rest, and lots of time spent with the woman curled up in the passenger seat. He gently nudged her shoulder. "We're here."

Jayne stretched and lifted her sunglasses. "Don't we have to stop by your parents' house to pick up the dogs?"

"My mom called earlier. She dropped them off a little while ago."

"I can't wait to see them." She climbed out of the car.

Zander rushed around the car and blocked her path. "Before we go in, I need to talk to you."

"All right." A frown wrinkled her brow.

He reached his hand toward hers. He'd never been nervous in all his years onstage. Yet, here with this woman, with this most important question, nerves jostled his stomach.

"I've never seen that look on your face before. What's wrong?"

"Nothing's wrong." His nerves settled a bit once he held her hand in his. He glanced over his shoulder at the house. On cue, Shredder and Patch came running toward them. Bow ties adorned their necks.

Jayne stooped to greet the dogs. Laughing, she touched Shredder's tie. "Well, someone dressed up for the occasion."

Zander fought to keep his voice casual, "Looks like there's a new tag hanging off of Patch's collar."

He took hold of Shredder while she stilled Patch's wiggling and peered at the tag he'd had Luke add that morning. Her eyes widened. "Zander."

He knelt beside her, grasped her hand and then repeated the words stamped on the metal heart. "Will you marry me?"

Mouth open, she gaped at him and her hand tightened around his.

He reached his other hand into his pocket and pulled out the ring he'd purchased the day before.

"Oh my God." Tears sparkled in her eyes like sunlight reflecting off the ocean.

"I love you. Because of you, I found what was missing in my life."

"I love you too. You gave me a family." She raised a shaky hand to cup his cheek.

He slipped the diamond on her finger. "You're the only one I want to start one with."

Nodding and crying, she pulled him closer and lifted her lips to his. He fisted his hand in her hair, holding her to him, holding onto his forever.

Applause and cheers spilled out from the open patio doors. Gasping, Jayne broke the kiss and looked up. His band mates, Irisa and Dom, his parents, some of the road crew, Chad, Kate, and Dalton joined them in the yard.

Zander grinned and pulled Jayne to her feet. Surrounded by love and celebration, wrapped around the woman he loved, his heart finally had everything it had been yearning for.

And with Jayne along for the ride, he'd have it all for a lifetime.

ABOUT THE AUTHOR

Susan Scott Shelley is an award-winning author of contemporary romance. For as long as she can remember, she has been in love with Love and all the sweeping grand gestures, heart-sighing moments, and quiet comforts it entails.

In addition to writing romances, she is also professional voiceover artist and enjoys lending her voice to a wide range of projects.

An unapologetic optimist, she believes life should be lived with laughter and a sense of wonder. Her favorite things include running, sports, hard rock and old Hollywood movies.

She lives in Philadelphia with her very own Superhero and spends her days writing about tough heroes, smart heroines, and love being the strongest magic there is.

For her newsletter, book information, and more, visit her website: SusanScottShelley.com.